RISE AND SHINE

THE STORY OF A GIRL WHO BELIEVED

KASHISH SANDHU

BlueRose ONE.com
Stories Matter
NewDelhi • London

BLUEROSE PUBLISHERS
India | U.K.

BlueRose ONE.com
Stories Matter
NewDelhi • London

For permissions requests or inquiries regarding this publication, please contact:

BLUEROSE PUBLISHERS
www.BlueRoseONE.com
info@bluerosepublishers.com
+91 8882 898 898
+4407342408967

ISBN: 978-93-6783-821-1

Cover design: Yash Singhal
Typesetting: Namrata Saini

First Edition: January 2025

Contents

Preface ... *iii*

Introduction ... *vii*

Genre ... *ix*

Dedicated to ... *xi*

What You will Get from This Book and How ... 1

A joyful life is your own creation and can not be copied from others ... 3

Life in a Small Village ... 5

Punctuality and discipline ... 9

Are you true to yourself ... 12

How we can identify people with their behaviors ... 15

Nothing is wrong or right, keep doing things ... 19

How to stop comparing yourself with other ... 23

How to be mentally Strong and utilize your potential at right place ... 27

How psychology work in your life ... 30

How to avoid negative people ... 32

Focus of one goal and never divert yourself ... 35

How to develop the power of being OK in any situations ... 37

About Author ... 39

Acknowledgment ... 41

Preface

This book is about the people who have dreams but somehow they think that they don't have enough sources to achieve them or don't have that much zeal to work on them or the surrounding environment is not favorable. We as a normal human being always try to put the blame of our failure on others but in reality we are the one who is responsible for it. This book will put a light on how to overcome this negative thought process, how to heal yourself if you get hurt because of someone, how to avoid negative people and why?, and real issues of life.

This is a story where a small village girl who doesn't have anything decides to do something great and worked on it dedicately. The book is for every age group. This book has very powerful ideas that will change someone's life drastically just by thinking in different ways.

Hard work is not enough, you have to think in a different way. You can change anything with your thought process, your mindset matters a lot. I believe that our thought process, the way we think, plays a very important role in our life.

If your mindset is negative and you always try to find out faults in everything and in everybody then for sure you will not reach anywhere and keep struggling in your life but instead of finding out mistake and blaming others, if you try to find out what are the things which you are lacking, why your are not able to achieve what exactly you want to achieve? Are you putting all your effort with great enthusiasm and dedication towards your goal ? What are the hindrances ?Are you true to yourself while speaking? If you know the answer to these questions, this is the first step towards your goal and you will surely get success in your life.

Success is not a fluke, you have to work hard, think positive, be consistent, be confident and committed to what exactly you want. Difficulties will come in everyone's life. You should not fluster and run away from it. Learn to face it and overcome it. she was quite an ambivert person but it never deteriorated her goals so she decided to discuss how she came over from a difficult situation, from a difficult place and a difficult in Environment to a convenient and happy environment.

Introduction

Being born in a small town, she always wants to get an exposure to the larger world. Coming from a very humble background, Parents were government Employees, they were three sisters and one brother, they had limited resources but that never deterred them especially her. Her extraordinary Journey from a small- town girl with a big dream to a passionate advocate for early childhood education and family well being. With a background in computer engineering and MBA in HR, She has successfully balanced her life and is now happy with her role as a dedicated mother.

She worked in many different organizations as she had to bear her living expenses and study as well. Her college education was self funded. She always had this feeling that a woman is the central pillar of a family hence one should be in a job which allows her to have a career as well as gives her enough time to bring up a happy family. She was very passionate about whatever she takes up. Now she is a mother of two beautiful children.

She has a very good understanding of how to contribute to child development at an early age. Understanding people is easy but understanding a child and their needs are complicated, So she decided to work on it and now she is a parenting coach and works on relationship management as well because both are internally connected. You will get to know more in my upcoming book soon.

Genre

It's a memoir, autobiography, story and some life experiences of an enthusiastic girl. When you share your true experiences of life, the struggle you made in your life or you saw people struggling around you but some of them landed up at a place where they are living a totally different life. Sharing experiences and changing the life of many who are suffering with the same kind of issues or may not be able to take the first step to come out of their comfort zone.

Dedicated to

I have dedicated this book to those who are struggling because of their thought process, their negative mindset, their low confidence to take decision for themselves, who keeps trying to make other happy at the cost of their happiness, who don't know how to live life for themselves, and would like to change their lifestyle, to fill their lives with positive energy or to get rid of some resistances like fear, doubts, jealousy, guilt, shame and regrets or some of them are those who have no courage to come out of it. They are the slave of their poor mindset, thought process. This book is the complete package for such people to improve them and get rid of all negativity.

What You will Get from This Book and How

Sometimes in our life we are so frustrated that we think nothing is going positive, I can't do anything. No one loves me, nothing is in my favor. We keep on blaming one or the other thing or person for our failures but when we get success very few of us appreciate the contribution of others.

This book will help you to understand how you can think positive and overcome your obstacles. How you can focus on your GOAL (going over always), How you can be happy with whatever you have, how to live for yourself not to please others because once you start living for yourself no one or nothing can stop you to be happy all the time. Be who you are and say what you feel, because those who mind don't matter, and those who matter don't mind so dont waste your time to please others especially who don’t appreciate you no matter if they are your close blood relatives, even your son or daughter.

Failure is an amazing teacher, don’t be afraid of being failure instead be afraid of not facing your fear of failure. Taking consistent action will lead anyone to success and a happy life. Always follow ACT which means Ambitious, Courageous and TRY thing, FAIL and again TRY. Learn from your failure and keep improving. Those who never fail in their life can't enjoy success.

You will learn how to be satisfied with whatever you have and keep working for more. Success doesn't mean you are completely satisfied. Happiness is from within even though you did not get whatever you want, you are happy. You can not get happiness with your success. Have you ever seen a fully satisfied person in your life? I am pretty sure NO

One day you get success, you celebrate it and the very next day you start working for your next goal. Life is like that. Keep moving and celebrate your next goal when you succeed. So to get happiness your success hardly matters. Happiness is always from within.

You won't be happy at the destination if you can't be happy during your journey.

A joyful life is your own creation and can not be copied from others

What will happen if you are part of a big family?

What if your parents have an attraction towards boys, not the girl child?

What if you think that your parents don't love you? Many times children thinks like that but

Life is too short to think about these questions, basically to lead a joyful life we should focus on our GOAL.

Going over all

Follow your Dreams, Figure out where you would to be, where you like to be doing, and then figure out what you need to do to get there. well said by Kennin M Sheldon

The Story is about an ambitious girl who was born in a middle class family. It was a hot summer day as u know in mountain sun is very harsh, a small girl was thinking about her future which she was unaware of! Life was very struggleful as in that era parents had many children.

Lovely dawn and looking towards the far far mountains, that little girl was thinking "

One day will come, she will see the world and she keeps on thinking about writing so many poems and stories.

"Dur wadiyon mein kahin hawa ke jhonke ne paigam bheja hai

Ye waqt ruk ja shyed ye khat kisi ne mere naam bhejha he

Rukna na tu, jhukhna na tu, es jamane ke dar se

Kayunki uparvale ne tujhe dekar ye kaam bhejha he

Karna he pura to lag ja aaj se hi es kaam par

Agar tum harogi nahi to ek din pahunch hi jaogi apne mukaam par"

It was a small village where one joint family lived. Early 90's people used to have many children so they also had four children. You know son means Pride for that era people as if they are truly blessed. They used to live in a beautiful house on the hill top. Time was flying and soon all children got married one by one. All were in some job no matter government or private.

Everyone had their own family and they were enjoying it in their own way. No one was so rich in that era especially in middle class families but still it always happened in Indian families to show off so many of them used to show off for their money or living standard.

Out of these four brothers one brother had three girls and one boy. All were good in study but few were ambitious but still felt the difference between boys and girls intentionally or unintentionally that had never deteriorated the ambition of these children. They continue to work on what exactly they are looking for and decide to achieve something different. If you think differently other than a crowd you would definitely be different than a crowd.

Opportunities are everywhere if you want to see and nowhere if you don't want to see it. life was full of ups and down but when you know you have to do this otherwise you cannot survive, you cannot change the world

Life in a Small Village

Living in the village life is beautiful but tough. Village offers a serene and tranquil environment, people are connected to each other and help each other and focus on basic community needs. It's a remarkable aspect of the village life people have strong community bonds. Most of the people depend on agriculture and they share things with each other without any cost. They have cultural richness, deeper connection with nature and celebrate all the festivals and traditions together. People live simple and content lives in a close knit community.

Earlier Schools were very far away, because of the mountain range there used to have harsh winters, crossing rivers and then going to school, sitting in the open hall for the education and when the weather was not good two classes had to sit together. You never know when the rain starts in hilly areas. You can not miss the school in the rain as well. Parents can't go behind the child to check if they went to school or not. Sometimes elder brothers or sisters are taking their siblings to school. I did this for my younger sister. Sometimes the school teacher who lives near your house will take all the small kindergarten children with her.

Students are self motivated else there is nothing to motivate them to study. If you are not motivated you are leading toward a life of laborers. All depends on the home environment, what type of parents do you have, If they are educated they will force their children to study and to get into some government job.

The Girl was so adamant about doing any government jobs because she has seen people who were doing government jobs need to live separately. Her understanding was that if you don't have a good family, not living together just for earning then life is useless. So she decided not to do a Government job.

She thinks that the most important challenge that a person faces is the mindset. Poverty, money, Home environment comes later. Challenges or failure are part of life and they help us to understand life better and help us to grow as a good human being, to make us stronger and lead us to solve greater challenges in future.

Poverty may be mental or material.

Mental poverty is the roadblock for growth. Its a lack of aspiration and ability to think about your future and your family's future.

Thought process plays an important role in all this. By cultivating positive thought, visualizing your goal and focusing on it means you are inviting the universe to be more kind to you and work for it. Its law of attraction. I strongly believe in it as your life is your thought process. You will lead your life the way you will think. Our mindset shapes our lives both internally and externally. Positive thought leads to positive outcome and happy and contented life but negative thought will create barriers and setbacks at every point of time. Our thoughts are blueprints of our reality but still sometimes people try to hide their true identity and try to show which actually they are not. Self Belief, mindfulness and gratitude towards others is the key to success.

You are the creator of your own destiny. Take responsibility for your work, decision, and life. If you want something in your life just start thinking and do not forget it even for a single day. Shift your thoughts, shift your mindset towards it, keep working on it and believe in yourself as power is within you. No one else can help you until you do.

This happens with her as well. As surrounded with people whose mindset is orthodox and she wanted to come out of it. Coming out from that tough environment you need to have a big heart and patience to listen to so many people. All will criticize you especially if you are a girl but who can stop dreamers!

It was not even the era of the internet, still these girls have high dreams."coming out of your comfort zone" It's very important that if you want to do something in your life and you're self motivated you need to come out of your comfort zone, that is what that small girl did!

After finishing her graduation when her parents did not give her money for further education she just left home and started a small job. She was studying as well as doing a job for her living. She and her three friends don't want to be overburden on their parents so they all came together, some with parents consent, some without. They became rebels to find out the path towards their Goal as they can't live the life of their age group in that area. They want something different, something great. Some of them want to become an IAS officer or engineer. All were helping each other in their bad times but never asked for money from their parents. Many people spoke about them and keep telling "these girls will never listen to anyone.

One lady said “ye to ambar mein ched karegi” means “this girl will make a hole in the sky” This was a very bad slang which she used for her.

Time was passing and they were working on their goal meanwhile all other girls got married then again one more challenge came “to get marry” but who has time to think about this these girls focused on their work and doubt they did not achieved so much but their hard work paid off and they are living a excellent life now which one can dream of.

Learning is that "You don't have to hold on to people who bring you down no matter how long you have known them for. "Because “when your nails Grow Long, you need to cut your nails, not your fingers” So do it at the right time.

Punctuality and discipline

Punctuality is very important in life, I am not saying people will not achieve anything if they are not punctual but yes they will not achieve what they really can achieve.

I have seen very talented people but they couldn't achieve many things just because they don't have discipline and punctuality in life. Make sure when you think something you just keep your focus .

When I finished my Diploma I wanted to go for higher education but due to my family condition I was not able to do that. Now I called it family condition but it was just a thought " Thought process of my Parents"

It was not about money but when you think that it's not possible, it will not be possible. Never allow people to rule you, just listen to them and do what is right for you. There is no need to be liked by everyone, people will hate you anyways no matter what you do for them. Not everyone will like you, some will love you, some will hate you, some will admire you, some will feel jealous of you, some will appreciate you, some will copy you silently and pretend that they are doing it themselves because they like it. There are many kinds of people in this world, it is really difficult to identify them but when you have a clear understanding about life you will come to know and can segregate them.

Punctuality and discipline will never come in a day, everyone needs to inculcate this from childhood. So it is the parents responsibility to help their child at a young age.

Changing some adults is difficult, you can only pretend to change, you will never change. We can not blame anyone if they are good behaved or they don't respect others because it's the result of the environment in which they were in their childhood. There is a saying "the apple doesn't fall far from the tree" so changing people later is difficult though not impossible. Children often inherit the characteristics of their parents.

Discipline doesn't mean to scold children, to be an authoritative, be so strict to the children, saying No all the time, Controlling them too much, giving punishment, loving them when they will listen to you, venting out your stress on children, commenting on their appearance or intelligence or comparing them with other children. By doing all this we are not teaching them respect but we are controlling them and this will not last for long, you are making them stubborn, you are not setting any standard but you are manipulating, you are becoming abusing and venting out your stress on them, comparison make their confidence low and it will affect their personality, they will feel low. You know,such children will later have no love and respect for you. They will be completely detached from you.

Discipline is something which comes from within, we just need to guide them. You can not teach discipline and punctuality to anyone until they are not self driven. You just need to help your child to be driven. Whatever they will do they should have a clear interest in it, focus should be clear, he needs to understand why he is doing this. I have seen many parents who want their children to be in the top ten but what is their contribution towards their children? Just money and anything materialistic they want, and continuous advice " keep studying, keep studying". They will never check what their children are studying. Do they need help ?Are they really studying or just opening the book and passing time?

Initial ten years of a child's life, if you are not deeply involved with your child you should not expect emotional connection with your child later. They will not remember what you have done for them, how much did you spend on them, how many toys you had purchased for them, What they will remember is, How much time did you spend with them, Did you tell them bedtime stories? Have you ever sat with them and watched some good movies of their interest? Have you ever gone with them to play badminton, soccer, tennis or for swimming? Basically how much time you are spending with our child is your wealth and insurance for future emotional well being. Because expecting too much without doing it for them in their childhood is just to find water in the desert. Their happiness for you is momentary and later they will speak as per their thought. You keep on doing for them they will worship you, just stop doing all those things for them immediately you will see their true faces. So better not spoil your life to make others happy. You can't make anyone happy if they don't want to be. Happiness is from within and that always comes from within.Struggle hard, understand what you want, work for it in spite of several failures and for sure you will get success. Even a happy life can not be without a measure of darkness and the word happy will lose its meaning if it is not balanced by sadness. Well said By Carl G Jung

Are you true to yourself

If you will get a new lease of life, would you like to live that?

Many people in this world are not true to themselves. They don't know what exactly they are looking for! They are not opinionated about their decision, their thought process but their thought changes as per the place, as per the environment, as per the people around them. They are slaves to situations.

Success is never a cakewalk to anyone, you need to work hard. Everyone wants success in their life, very few work on it. So the main goal of life, be true to yourself. Whatever you are thinking, should come out of your mouth. Sometimes unknowingly we make so many mistakes and we know that we are doing wrong but we have no courage to admit it. So we keep on telling lies to hide that particular part .

These kinds of people want to please others at any cost no matter if they are hurting other sentiments. They will not be happy themselves and create problems in someone else's life as well unknowingly. These people will always be in pain and always blame others for their misery. One can categorically change their life if they want to be by doing small changes in their thought process. Just to be true to themself no matter what.

Few children are over pampered and parents are mollycoddling them after they become adults as well. They keep on shouting and anger is their tool to get the work done from others though they don't know that they are punishing themselves sometimes because of their own mistake or sometimes because of others.

I have met many peculiar people who do not say things just because they are afraid of losing them. They are arrogant and rigid to accept the truth and to hide the truth they keep on telling lies and fooling others. Stop hanging out with such people who are snooty.

To be happy in your life remember few tips:

1. Stop snooping in someone's life, Your life is great, enjoy every moment of it.
2. Sometimes life malfunctions, don't worry, It's a matter of time and it will pass.
3. In your relationship don't be SIMP, Be ALPHA. SIMP people will always have a chance to get cheated by others. Don't leave such a room in your life.Just live and let live.
4. You will meet many oddballs in your life, ignore them if they are not important in your life. Don't waste your time on them.
5. Sometimes we fluster, what to do and what not. In this situation, think calmly and take your time. Do not do anything in a hurry.
6. You should not rest on your laurels, because life is a continuous learning process so keep learning.
7. Your life will be in jeopardy if you let it be led by others.
8. You should take a punt to start anything new which you like. This will lead to two options: either you will

get success or you will fail. Both have learning and you should enjoy both

9. Do all these in a nick of time else you will keep thinking why I did not work on this on time? Because not everyone is mature enough to get over that feeling. So anything you want to do kick start it.
10. Last but not list, Be a glow Getter not Glow Fader.

How we can identify people with their behaviors

Identifying someone's behavior is a talent. These days you will hardly find people who genuinely care about you and want to help you.

To understand people you should understand yourself profusely. This is the problem in most people ,we don't understand ourselves and we try to change others. We should be observant all the time and keep listening to people. One mantra of learning well is listening more and more. When you speak we give the knowledge to other people and gain nothing but when we listen we learn new things no matter good or bad. It's very important to see bad things to understand them deeply. Think if nothing bad happens to you in your life how would you know what is bad?

These days we are pampering our children and immediately solving their problems without letting them try. Let them try, let them find out the way to resolve their own issues. Make them strong, confident and independent instead of weak, lack of confidence, looser and freeloader.

One thing which we need to make clear to this generation is, to be your own judge, don't let anyone lead your life. Your parents are the one who genuinely care about you, want to see you at some level rest all will be opportunist. All bow down to success so just focus on you and your career. Money and people will come to you automatically.

Sometimes we like to live a lavish life and for that we keep on making mistakes, Looking at people and just trying to copy them or follow them blindly without knowing the details of how they reached there? Is everything real or just for show off?

Have you seen people fighting and suddenly they saw someone clicking their picture? They act as if nothing happened and show in the picture that they are the one whom people should admire, wanted to live like them, wanted to know how they are so lucky. But the reality is something else. I have seen many cases who seem to be ideal pairs/couples but with zero understanding.

One should understand that everyone's life is unique and we need to focus on our only. There are certain responsibilities, understand that and keep working on yourself for better you.Social media is a blessing as well as curse both. If you use it with a positive mindset, it will be a blessing as it has every kind of knowledge but if you keep looking at others life, how they are living, where they are visiting, what type of house they have?What their parents have given to them ?What and how much wealth does he has? What gift did her husband gave? Etc etc so many comparisons, you know you will lead a miserable life.

I know many of my friends who have no understanding with their wife/husband but when they come out publicly, people would love to be that type of couple.

Understanding your partner or people is very important. What is your thought process? Sometimes we are influenced by others so much that we don't even know that whatever we are doing is not our own wish, thought process. Someone else is controlling us.

While some pain is probably inevitable in all relationships or parts of life, successful people are the ones who are able to forgive and forget. Understand the situation and try to forgive people and move ahead. I know it is difficult but if we are able to do so, believe me we will achieve whatever we want to achieve. Just give it a try and do not let anyone control you.

You can avoid people in many ways:

1. Do not sit at the table where someone is gossiping about others because when you leave that table you will be the topic.
2. Do not ask anything from your partner just because your friend got it, ask if you really like it and need it.
3. Remember what you will do, your children will learn and later they will make a family so your contribution with your behavior at this point of time is so valuable for an upcoming family.
4. Be happy whatever you have, people have everything other than happiness and satisfaction so if you're happy and satisfied, you are the richest among all.
5. Give lots of time to your loved one because time is the only thing which will not come back.
6. Understand people before making friends with them, do not stick to your blood relation.Sometimes they are worse than some strangers. So understand people and give them the place that they deserve in your life not because it's compulsory due to some blood relation.
7. Avoid split personality people. They will be good at your face and bitch about you behind your back. Just check who is very sweet to everyone, they are

dangerous, cunning and selfish people. No one in this world can be good to everyone, disagreement will always be there, if someone claims "everyone loves me" "everyone likes me or good to me" I have no problem with anyone, that's the person you should avoid. These types of people keep using you by saying sugary words so be careful from such people.

Nothing is wrong or right, keep doing things

Sometimes in life we are influenced by negative people and start diverting ourselves. This could be due to peer pressure, society, relatives or anyone in your life. For doing right thing you need not take anyone 's approval. Just try it once and you will not lose anything. There are two outcomes: either you will fail or succeed but you will not lose anything for sure. So go and start it today categorically.

Many people will push you back and try to stop you in many ways. You should act like water at that time. No matter how many mountains or bushes will come in his way it keeps on flowing and making its way. Similarly in our life we should keep working and not waste our time on regrets of failures and what people think about our work.

Many of them will just come to break your confidence and don't want to see you rise. Be silent and keep working. Basically don't waste your life pleasing useless people no matter if they are your blood relations as well. Nothing is wrong when we are doing the right things. This is the biggest problem of this Era"Kya Kahenge Log ye Sabse Bada Rog "

Research indicates that most of us are overthinkers. over thinking drains us, contributes to severe depression, anxiety and many mental health issues. Over-thinking is when you get into the way of what you want. When we over things we change to get stuck in a negative thought loop called rumination. Instead of taking action we keep on thinking and cannot take any logical decision.

Over thinking is directly related to:-

- Depression and fatigue.
- Can create the disease like in insomnia
- Anxiety disorders
- Negativity
- Increased risk drug and alcohol abuse
- Suicide attempts
- Bad decision making
- Low quality social relationship

Sometimes we think about our past and future but we forget to think about what is happening in our current time, our present . For example, we think if someone is not talking to you you waste time thinking why he is not talking to me? Did I do something wrong to him? By thinking like this you are just wasting your present where you can do something great. Past is the past, don't try to change it.

You are trying to improve your past mistakes and do whatever is possible to rectify those mistakes. Such kind of people will never focus on their current blessing and keep crying about whatever has happened in the past.

Something which is out of your control like the economy or the Global crisis or someone else's problems, do not waste time on such things but many people keep on wasting time on it. Before thinking about all these things or other problems, you should think about what is happening in your life and your current family. Remember if you can't make your family happy then you cannot make anyone happy in this world. Just start making changes from your family. If you are making your family members happy then you can make anyone happy in this world.

Don't feel bad or tense if someone else has what you wanted and you are not able to take that instead work hard and get it. Always ask yourself what and if. Like every time when we think that the other person has so much and we don't have, instead of this if you think that whatever we have is more than enough and keep on working for the best Nothing can make you happier than if you have a level headed mindset.

Every time you think negatively, ask multiple IFs and "What" from you. There are many types of people who are particularly over-thinkers.

The first one is the **Shy type,** the shy type people think when they go to sleep they replay everything whatever has happened during the day time and analyze for what they were worried about, what others will think about them? and whether they have made a good impression or not?

Second is the **insecure type** of people. These types of people are worried about the circumstances and they mostly have sleepless nights. They keep on thinking and disturbing others. They have low self esteem and are constantly worried about their job,their family, their work pressure, there surroundings.They always think negatively and they are insecure from everywhere they want to copy people.

Third type of people are **highly sensitive** people. These are the people who have a mix of insecure people and shy people. They are sensitive to small-small things, they feel bad or good, they tend to have a stronger emotional reaction, more compassion and greater sensitivity to criticism. They can't handle the activities easily and when somebody is present with them they become so happy.

The Fourth type of people are **confident** people. These kinds of people are highly successful. They are self aware people and know exactly how to handle different situations no matter if it is good or bad. These kind of people know how to express, don't stress themselves, don't waste their time on non productive things and negative people.They make sure that everything should be communicated in a clear way and with no chaos.

How to stop comparing yourself with other

Sometimes we keep comparing ourselves with others which always leads us to depression and anxiety. It takes control over your own life and starts degrading your lifestyle.You should believe in your capabilities and how you can stop yourself by comparing yourself with others. Few things which you can keep in your mind to identify to avoid the comparison:-

- Identify the people or event or prompt or your surrounding comparative behavior and write down your negative thoughts so that you can limit those thoughts
- Make a list of your strength and weakness, start writing a journal everyday what you are doing from morning to evening
- Make a list of positive things happening in your life and read it before sleeping.
- Set Screen time limit for your social media account because social media is the culprit. It's good and bad for both those who are using it in a positive way. It's good for them and those who don’t understand, leave them.
- Always say some positive things about yourself like I am a genuine person, I am a courageous person, I am an incredible person.

- Give a positive affirmation to yourself that you can do anything in this world. that you are the most intelligent person.
- While listing the thing in your general, explain how they impact on your life in detail for example if you are working in the ground or if you jogging in the park you can express how you are grateful to your health that you are able to Jog, how you are grateful to God that you are able to walk because you have two feet, Be grateful to the people around you.
- Practice gratitude everyday, pay attention and give compliments, receive compliments and you can give compliments to random people as well.
- Kindness always returns kindness, nature will give you what you will give to others by doubling it.
- Keeping a gratitude general can increase your chance to overcome comparison. You can read this everyday and try to identify what you have to do and what you have to get rid of.
- Always appreciate others instead of feeling jealous of them. For example, your friend is a highly achieving person, so you must consider that network in a positive way and use their successful stories in a positive way. For example if you are going to a gym instead of seeing other people's fitness level and feeling jealous you should try to do what they are doing and ask them the Mantra how they actually did it. In this way you will learn something instead of just thinking and thinking and feeling jealous or inferior. Success is shabby, chaotic so be careful while thinking, be consistent and keep working. "Fail fast and fail forward" Anything that is scaring your do it

fast, quick. Use trial and error method. Doubt, fear, jealousy, comparison, guilt, insecurities and regret are the resistances, get over them as soon as possible.

- You can use these motivations to make changes in your life. You can change your eating habits ,your dressing sense, your thinking.
- Instead of focusing on your weakness try to focus on your strength because you can make a list of where you were in the first week, what you have achieved
- Track your progress so that you can see how you are moving forward towards your goal, focus on your goal and not on the people.
- The way you will focus on yourself nobody else can do that. You should judge yourself with your own standard and never let anyone judge you. Remember that everyone has a different level of Revelation that impacts their life.
- Everyone's struggles are different. Enjoy your struggle of life because your journey is unique so be patient and focus on your goal do not compare yourself with anyone, just try to find out how the other person is able to achieve and why not me, when you start thinking like this believe me you will get your answer and you will start working towards positive and start seeing the results.
- Replace negative thoughts with positive ones, be a good friend of yourself, take control of your own life, do not let anyone take control of your life.
- At the end of the day you know you are the best so make decisions for yourself, not for anyone else.

- To overcome comparison, you can't stop thinking about other instead of using other people as a benchmark for your success use comparison to help, to structure your goal, to focus for your improvement and to focus on your healthy and happy life because in this Era people will get lots of filthy the money but they will not have happiness.

How to be mentally Strong and utilize your potential at right place

Are you mentally strong?

Some people quickly bounce back from personal failure and setbacks. On the other hand some find it very very difficult when life knocks them down. Are you easily handing it up or are you adapting to the circumstances and compromise? Are you finding the difficulties and lack of confidence in your ability to deal with the challenges?

If you are in any of the categories, you will always have the opportunities where you can overcome any situation in your life. There are many practical strategies to building mental resilience. It is a quality which you learn with time, with interaction, with the people and experiences. What you are doing in your day today depends on the circumstances or anything that is happening in your life like you are losing your job or death of your loved one, end of relationship or you got some failure in any of your favorite projects.

You can rise and come back even stronger than you are before. It totally depends upon how positively you are thinking about this situation. Mental strength is the capacity of an individual to deal with any situation effectively. It always depends upon the habit that breaks mental muscle, your thought process. It also involves giving up bad habits and holding you back in a positive attitude.

When you are mentally strong you are using your true potential. You can replace your negative thoughts with positive and more realistic thoughts will come. You will be able to control your emotions and you can take positive action. You can inculcate in your children at the right age so that when they develop as an adult they will be easily able to handle such situations.

Let your child make mistakes ,mistakes are an inevitable part of learning. Help your child to understand that mistakes are very very important to learn anything new. They should not be embarrassed or ashamed about getting something wrong. Develop a habit of healthy talk. If your child has done something wrong you should talk to him and explain why it has happened and what are the pros and cons of this? and how can you deal with this situation in your life?

Encourage your child to face the fear in their life, it will help him to gain invaluable confidence. This is the way where you are helping your child to step outside of his comfort zone and face the fears.

Sometimes you will be in an uncomfortable situation where you are seeing that your child is struggling to get something. Many of us don't want our children to struggle but we want to give them whatever they want immediately.

To make our children's strong we should stop doing all this things because if you are not teaching them how to come out from the difficult situation then tomorrow they will come to us and that time it will be very difficult for us to handle situation so let your children deal with this situation on their own and can help the children to build their mental strength. It will build their character.

You can help your children by instilling values of honesty, doing your things yourself, learning Exercise of Practical life (EPL) and compassion which creates learning opportunities that reinforce these values regularly.

Help your children to understand gratitude, encourage them to practice it on a regular basis. Gratitude helps us to keep things in perspective even more challenging. It's time to raise your child mentally strong. Children should understand and take responsibility for their own actions or mistakes. It is also part of building mental strength.

Children learn from their parents and surrounding environment, if they see people keep on blaming others and don't take responsibility for their actions, they will also learn the same. Instead of taking responsibility they will try to impose that mistake/blame on others either on their parents, teacher or on their friends.

It is very important to help your children to take responsibility for their actions. If your child is trying to blame others just listen to him carefully and then explain how and why you should not do that. You should give reason to your children why and what is important .

Help your child to control their emotions because children who know better how to control their emotions can prepare themselves in a better way to deal with ups and downs in their life. You should be a role model for your child.

How psychology work in your life

Psychology plays a very important role in your life, what we think in our life will surely happen. It can be fun and fascinating or it can also be frustrating. It all depends upon how we think and how we receive things. I can say with personal experience that if you have a strong goal you can achieve anything in your life.

To achieve something you need a strong determination no matter in which school or what type of school you are studying. You need to be very particular about what you are actually looking for in your life and consistently focus on it and keep working on it. Life is always what we think about.

Psychology plays a vital role in everyone's life. Your thought process will decide what will be your future. Nothing is impossible and if we work on this principle that anything is possible then we can achieve anything and that is all dependent upon our mind set.

There are two types of people, one who thinks that I can do it and the other one who thinks that it is really hard. Both types of people have a different mindset and lifestyle. I believe that if you work hard in your early age you will get a good life in your later age but if you did not work hard in the beginning of your life then definitely you will lead a miserable life or struggleful life. I have seen many people who had a very good life during their early childhood or early School and later lead to struggles in their life.

Sometimes we think that we should give everything to our children and they should not face any difficulties. Children become habitual of this and in the later stage when they reach the 20's and start earning or start their career or somehow they will not get the job because of their poor education they will find difficulty to lead such a luxurious life. They start blaming their parents, relatives, friends or the close ones who are successful in their life. Because of their poor and negative mindset they think that it is the responsibility of parents to give these things to us and when they are unable to give then they feel bad and start behaving differently, sometimes even scold them and blame them for their failure. Sometimes they start hitting their parents or sometimes they think if they are not helping means they are their enemy.

It is just your mind set which leads to success or failure. You should consider yourself like water. Which can flow between the stones or the mountain as well and make its way easily. If you know how to achieve your goal no matter how difficult it is you will find the way to achieve it if you are consistently working on it and focusing on your goal. Here psychology plays a very important role. Sometimes when we have a positive mindset, we can do things in an easy way.

These types of techniques we can use for our children also to make them understand new things. I am telling you with my personal experience that I am a strong believer of nature and psychology. I believe if we think about something it will definitely happen in our life depending upon how strongly we feel it. If you want to achieve something in your life, be consistent, make a note and read it everyday in the morning and remind yourself that this is what you actually have to do. You will definitely achieve that because you are constantly focusing on that particular goal.

How to avoid negative people

To Lead a peaceful life it is very important to have a positive environment around you but it is not possible all the time because everywhere people always focus on other things. What are you doing? How are you doing? and why are you doing it?

These days people have everything but they don't have peace of mind, they want to earn lots of money, they want a big house, they want good education for the children no matter what it will cost the mental health of the child.

Sometimes we become so emotional, emotions are the raw material of our thought process, thought factory or our mind. Whatever we will feel, the outcome will come accordingly. We should fill our life with positive emotions like courage, confidence, faith, hope, enthusiasm, love, peace, joy, compassion, forgiveness, kindness and optimism. And Avoid negative emotions like fear, worry, hate, anger, jealousy, revenge, pessimism and doubt sink in. We will definitely lead a happy life. You need not be good to everyone, it's not required.

I have read somewhere that "too goodness is a sickness." It's true. You know no one will value you if you are too good to everyone whenever there will be something they will put it on the people.

Sometimes we keep on searching for happiness at the wrong place, happiness is within us. Positive emotions and negative emotions are the state of mind, your thought process or the environment. The way you think will change your life. People think it happens because of someone else. No, No it's your Karma. You can hide anything from people but not with nature.

Many times in your family you face such an issues that people spread negativity about you and if you don't stop them they keep on doing. Once you know what are the things that make us unhappy we must transcend them in order to live a life of joy, bliss and peace.

If you are a negative thinker you will surely lead a miserable life. People who are negative thinkers will never think positively, always blame others, do not respect others, not be grateful to anyone no matter how much someone will do, they are always ungrateful.

Thinking positive itself is a blessing. You will always choose everything wisely and avoid negativity. It is not important how many friends, relatives or people around you, it's important who all are available when you need them. Rest all are opportunist.

Everything change as per your thinking, Mindset plays a very important role. Even if we see in our history like Ram and Ravana, Ravana was very intelligent, rich, he had everything, all lavish things, he could control the planetary positions at his will, owned pushpak Viman (a flying chariot) which he won from his step brother Kuber. He was an excellent veena player but he had a negative attitude which led to his defeat from Rama. Rama was not that powerful, he didn't have that many lavish things but what he had, was his positive mindset, his positive attitude.

Mindset is such a powerful tool to achieve anything. What your life is and what your life will be all depends on mindset.

Focus of one goal and never divert yourself

The first thing which you should learn in your life is to stay focused on your GOAL. The day you divert yourself, you will lose everything. Focus means " Follow One Course Until Success". So make your mind and think, what you want in your life, you will get it.

There was a story behind it.

One small girl always wanted to do something great. She saw her surroundings and found that this environment was not made for her. She started working on it and kept the Goal in her mind that she will do something and will not live like others are living here in a small town. She silently kept working on it.

So many struggles, obstacles came in her way but her focus was very very clear, Not to stay at that place, to be independent. She worked in MNC's, did self study , never overburdened on her parents and married to a well educated person and living a life the way she wanted to be. This is the life she has created with her thought process. Nothing is impossible in this world .

Many more people can change their life. You will lead a kind of life as your thought process. If your thought process is positive and progressive, you will achieve anything in this world.

Everyone has their own problem, their own struggle, none of them are the same for all. If you are talking about boys, they have the responsibility from the beginning that if you are a boy you need to do this or that. Many social obligations and responsibilities. If you are a girl you also have hell lot of responsibilities, don't do this, don't do that, walk like that, talk like that. Etc But why?

All should do their work and understand their responsibilities, this is how we can run a beautiful life. But some parents are not able to make a clear decision and keep so many if and what then what should you do.?

These are the rights of the children so we should speak about it but if it doesn't turn out believe me nothing bad will happen. The money which is from your sweat will only give you a reward. If you get it, welcome if not Leave it. Karama has all records and all have to serve their karma here only. Karma has no timetable, understand it or not.

Do not hesitate to appreciate anyone who helps you, did something good for you but don't forget who is there with you in your bad time. They are your real well wishers. Ignore their small small mistakes and enjoy.

If you are doing good to people and they are returning nothing as good what you have to do, remember that we all came with empty handed and will leave empty handed and again

Return to the title" just Focus on your goal and never divert yourself".

How to develop the power of being OK in any situations

Sometimes people are not happy with their life, not just because they are having struggles in their life but because of others' happiness like why they are better than me and keep cursing others for their miseries. They always focus on money and try to extract in whichever way from everywhere.

On the other hand if you learn to control your brain to be ok in every situation, you will become a strong person and no one can divert you from your goal.

Few people know that whatever has happened in their life was totally their mistake but they always keep blaming others for that. Such people can never live a happy life and they keep on struggling.

Money is something but not everything.

Living life to the fullest and in a happy way is the key to a meaningful life. What if you have lots of money but no happiness, what will you do with that money? Anyhow, one day everyone will die.

Sometimes we focus on money, properties and so many materialistic things but we forget to live life. By the time people die they have everything whatever they thought, like saved money, worked hard, have lots of properties, financial freedom and get retire with huge money but what they loose, is their life, their relations, they don't have memorable experiences as they kept on working hard for money or to make someone else happy or some other purpose.

It's OK to be a bad person than a dead person. You know who don't react either have reached the top of spirituality or they are dead souls. I always believed that do not start anything negative, fight or any situation with others, just let it. But if someone starts it from their side do not feel fear, handle it and make sure it ends from your side.

Okay, how we can be okay in every situation this is really a difficult task of today's era you cannot be okay in every situation but you can try to overcome that situation and try to handle that situation in a positive way whenever someone is putting you down or life is putting you down," Are you quick to pick yourself up and adopt to the circumstances that whatever has happened it's ok or you over think and get into depression anxiety and mental health issues it all depend upon how you think about life it shows your ability to deal with the challenges". You should be mentally strong.

You should remember the force "C's" **Control Commitment Changes and Confidence.**

When you know how to take control over the situation and how to be committed to overcome that situation and how to adapt the changes whatever has happened in your life then you can overcome anything in your life. To gain something all yourself to see the world from a different perspective sometime we see the world what is in front of us or what our parents are showing us but in this technology Era we should broaden our perspective in a different way. It's okay to be not okay sometimes.

About Author

Kashish Sandhu, being born in a small town, always wanted to get an exposure of the larger world. Coming from a very humble background, Parents were government Employees, we are three sisters and one brother, we had limited resources but that never deterred us especially me. My extraordinary Journey from a small- town girl with a big dream to a passionate advocate for early childhood education and family well being. With a background in computer engineering and MBA in HR from Symbiosis Pune, I have successfully balanced a thriving career with my role as a dedicated mother.

Prior to marriage I worked in many different organizations as I had to fulfill my living expenses because I do not want to overburden my parents, I joined MNC EXCEL Services and later did MBA HR from Symbiosis pune which was self funded. I always had this feeling that a woman is the central pillar of a family hence I should be in a job which allows me to have a career as well as gives me enough time to bring up a happy family. I worked 4 years in the MNC & Recruitment industry (especially for US recruitment). I am very much passionate about whatever I take up.

Now I am a mother of two beautiful children. My husband and I decided to divide the work. So he is working and I am taking care of the children which I believe is a tough and tedious job.

After having my first child I decided to gain knowledge about how to contribute in child development at an early age. My profession was Human Resource Management. I can understand people but understanding a child and his needs was out of the question, So i decided to study more about it and did a course from IMTC bangalore. It was quite an intense course but interesting. Since I was not doing a job, I decided to work on it more and it became my passion. Now I am a parenting coach and work on relationship management as well because both are internally connected. You will get to know more in my upcoming book soon.

Acknowledgment

Thanks to all my friends, family and neighbors. Its because of you all that I was able to find the truth within myself. Thank you for taking me out of my comfort zone. Some people will do it with positive force, some do with negative. It is important to know everything.

Thanks to my teacher, My mentor, My Mom and dad. My sister and my one and only one brother who is truly an inspiration for all of us. I would like to thank three most important persons in my life, My two beautiful children who were always with me on my journey and I get motivated just by seeing their cute faces. Special thanks to my backbone who is my Husband who is such a supportive, level headed person and gave me freedom to do what I want to do. We are strong pillar for each other with great understanding. We both work as a team and focus on our responsibilities in a better way.

You all are the reason today I am able to write this book and try to help others how to overcome difficult situations in your life. Your life is your, no one can make it better than you. You are the creator of your life, Positive and negative forces will always be there.

Without any of you, this book would not be in existence. Thanks you for everything.

The Heart's Trilogy

Three Shades of Romance

BOOKS CLINIC PUBLISHING

Published by Booksclinic Publishing
Empowering Authors, Inspiring Readers
Booksclinic Publishing
Bilaspur, Chhattisgarh, India
Website: www.booksclinic.com
Email: booksclinicpublishing@gmail.com

SKU Code: 2201
ISBN: 978-93-5823-168-7
Edition Details:
First Edition: [March, 2025]
Genre: Fiction
₹: 230/-

Credits
Cover Design: Aryan Dhiwar
Interior Design: Love Thawait

Publisher's Note
Booksclinic Publishing is dedicated to empowering authors and connecting them with over 20 lakh readers globally. The opinions and ideas expressed in this book are those of the author and do not necessarily reflect the views of the publisher.

For permissions, bulk orders, or author inquiries, please contact:
Email: booksclinicpublishing@gmail.com | **Phone: 9109669968**

Discover more inspiring stories at www.booksclinic.com

Printed in India

THE HEART'S TRILOGY

THREE SHADES OF ROMANCE

SOUMEN SENGUPTA

INDEX

The Midnight Letter

Chapter	*Title*	*Page*
1.	*The Antique Desk*	*1*
2.	*The Letters of Jules*	*4*
3.	*Midnight at the Clock Tower*	*8*
4.	*Echoes of the Past*	*12*
5.	*Unravelling the Threads*	*16*
6.	*The Secrets Beneath the Stone*	*20*
7.	*The Clock Tower's Secret*	*25*
8.	*The Awakening of Love*	*29*
9.	*The Echoes of Tomorrow*	*33*
10.	*The Final Letter*	*38*
11.	*Beyond the Clock*	*42*
12.	*A New Beginning*	*46*
13.	*Echoes of the Past*	*51*
14.	*A New Beginning*	*55*

The Quiet Goodbye

1.	*A Meeting in Exile*	*63*
2.	*Letters Begin – Life in Vienna*	*66*
3.	*Unspoken Truths*	*70*
4.	*Between the Lines*	*74*
5.	*Echoes of the Heart*	*78*
6.	*Across the Silence*	*82*
7.	*The Quiet Between Us*	*87*
8.	*The Unspoken Truth*	*91*
9.	*The Thread That Ties Us*	*95*
10.	*The Quiet Goodbye*	*99*

Canvas of The Heart

Chapter	*Title*	*Page*
1.	*The Quiet Village*	***105***
2.	*Harish's Dilemma*	***107***
3.	*The Unexpected Arrival*	***110***
4.	*A Day in Sundarvan*	***113***
5.	*A Shared Smile*	***117***
6.	*The Seeds of Affection*	***120***
7.	*The Festival of Lights*	***123***
8.	*Whispers of the Heart*	***124***
9.	*The Storm Within*	***127***
10.	*The Confession*	***130***
11.	*The Silent Storm*	***134***
12.	*The Slow Healing*	***138***
13.	*The First Signs of Change*	***142***
14.	*Secrets Unveiled*	***146***
15.	*The Truth Unfolds*	***151***
16.	*A Moment of Reflection*	***156***
17.	*A Step Toward Trust*	***160***
18.	*A Test of Faith*	***163***
19.	*A Leap of Faith*	***167***

THE MIDNIGHT LETTER

Chapter 1
THE ANTIQUE DESK

The cobblestone streets of Colmar glistened with the remnants of an afternoon rain. Camille Dupont adjusted her scarf against the crisp autumn air as she wandered through the bustling flea market, her eyes scanning rows of trinkets and treasures. A struggling writer in her late twenties, Camille had spent weeks battling a creative drought. She hoped this market, with its charming chaos, might hold the spark she needed to reignite her imagination.

She turned a corner and stopped in her tracks. There, tucked between a stack of faded books and a wrought-iron lamp, stood a desk. It was modest but elegant, its dark wood polished smooth, save for a few scratches that hinted at its age. The brass handles on the drawers gleamed faintly in the fading sunlight. Something about it called to her—perhaps it's quiet dignity, or the way it seemed to whisper of untold stories.

"Beautiful, isn't it?" The vendor, a wiry man with a weathered face, approached her. "Late 19th century. Found it in an old estate near here. Solid craftsmanship."

Camille ran her fingers along the edge of the desk, feeling its cool surface. "How much?" she asked, her voice laced with both excitement and hesitation.

"For you, mademoiselle, a fair price," the vendor said with a grin, naming a sum that made her wince. After a bit of haggling, Camille managed to negotiate it down to an amount that left her wallet significantly lighter but her heart lighter still.

With the help of a delivery service, the desk arrived at her tiny apartment later that evening. Camille cleared a space by the window, positioning the desk where she could look out at the town square while she worked. The desk fit perfectly, as though it had been waiting for her all along.

As she cleaned it, Camille noticed the faint scent of lavender emanating from the wood, as if it still carried traces of its past life. She opened the drawers, finding nothing but dust and an old ink stain in one corner. When she pulled open the bottom drawer, it stuck momentarily before giving way with a soft creak. She frowned, running her hand along its interior. Her fingers brushed against something—a small, uneven ridge at the back.

Her curiosity piqued, Camille grabbed a flashlight and peered inside. There, hidden in the shadowy depths, was a panel that didn't quite align with the rest of the wood. With a gentle push, the panel slid free, revealing a narrow compartment. Inside lay a bundle of yellowed papers tied together with a faded blue ribbon.

Her heart quickened as she carefully removed the bundle and untied the ribbon. The papers were letters, their edges brittle with age. The handwriting was elegant and flowing, each line written with precision and care. Camille held the first letter to the light and began to read.

My Dearest Élise,

There are no words to describe the fire you have ignited within me. Each moment without you feels like an eternity, and yet, it is the thought of you that sustains me through these endless days. I long for the night when we will meet under the clock tower, where time itself will bear witness to our love.

Yours eternally,
Jules

Camille's breath hitched. The words were raw, filled with a passion that seemed to leap from the page. She turned to the next letter, then the next, each one painting a vivid picture of a love both fierce and fragile. Yet, as she read on, a sense of unease settled over her. The letters spoke of longing, of obstacles, of a promise to meet—but there was no resolution.

Who were Jules and Élise? Why had these letters been hidden away? And what had become of the lovers whose story now lay in her hands?

Setting the letters down, Camille leaned back in her chair, her mind racing. This was no ordinary desk. It was a portal to a mystery—a story waiting to be told. Little did she know, her discovery would change her life forever.

Chapter 2
THE LETTERS OF JULES

The soft morning light streamed through Camille's apartment window, painting the antique desk in warm hues. Camille sat with a steaming cup of coffee, the letters spread before her like fragile pieces of a puzzle. She had spent the entire night immersed in them, unable to stop reading. Every word seemed to breathe life into a story that had been buried for over a century.

She picked up the next letter, her fingers trembling slightly as she unfolded it. The paper was delicate, its edges frayed, and the ink had faded to a soft sepia tone.

My Dearest Élise,

It has been days since I last saw your face, yet it feels like an eternity. Your absence is a wound that refuses to heal. I write this with the hope that these words will reach you as my heart does—steadfast and true. I cannot wait for the day when the world will no longer stand between us.

The clock tower shall be our witness. Midnight, my love. There, under its shadow, I shall wait for you. Whatever may come, I will wait.

Forever yours,
Jules

Camille's heart ached as she read the words. Jules' longing was palpable, his devotion unwavering. But there was something haunting about the letters—an undercurrent of desperation that made her chest tighten.

She placed the letter aside and reached for another, its folds worn as though it had been opened and closed countless times.

My Dearest Élise,

The thought of you sustains me in ways nothing else can. Yet, I must admit, my fears grow with each passing day. The obstacles before us seem insurmountable, but I cling to the hope that love will prevail. Do not let doubt cloud your heart, my Élise. Trust in me as I trust in you.

Midnight, beneath the clock tower. There, we will defy the world.

Yours eternally,
Jules

Camille leaned back in her chair, overwhelmed. The letters were filled with a love so profound it felt almost otherworldly. But they also raised questions she couldn't ignore. Why had these letters been hidden? Why had Jules and Élise needed to defy the world to be together? And most importantly, what had happened to them?

Her curiosity gnawed at her. She glanced out the window, where the clock tower loomed in the distance, its spire reaching toward the sky. The letters had mentioned it repeatedly—midnight under the clock tower, the promise of a love fulfilled.

Unable to resist the pull of the mystery, Camille gathered the letters and slipped them into a notebook. She needed answers, and the first step was learning more about Jules and Élise.

The town library was a quiet, unassuming building nestled between two rows of timber-framed houses. Camille

stepped inside, the faint smell of old books and polished wood welcoming her. She approached the front desk, where an elderly librarian peered over her glasses.

"How can I help you?" the librarian asked.

"I'm looking for any historical records or archives related to the clock tower," Camille said. "Specifically, anything from the early 1900s."

The librarian's eyebrows arched slightly. "Ah, the clock tower. Quite the landmark, isn't it? We do have some records. You'll find them in the local history section."

Camille thanked her and made her way to the section, where dusty volumes and bound newspapers awaited. She began sifting through the materials, searching for anything that might mention Jules, Élise, or the letters.

Hours passed, and just as she began to lose hope, she stumbled upon an old newspaper clipping. The headline read: "Tragic Accident in Colmar: Young Woman Dies Near Clock Tower."

Her breath caught as she read the article. A young woman named Élise Moreau had died in an accident near the clock tower on the night of October 12, 1903. The details were sparse, but it mentioned a collision with a horse-drawn carriage.

Camille's mind raced. Could this be the same Élise? The timing and location matched the letters. If so, then Jules' love story had ended in heartbreak—and his midnight promise had never been fulfilled.

That night, back in her apartment, Camille laid the letters out once more. The pieces were beginning to fall into place,

but the picture they painted was tragic. Élise had died before she could meet Jules under the clock tower.

But why, then, had Jules continued to write to her? Why had these letters been hidden in the desk for so long?

Camille stared at the clock tower through her window, its silhouette illuminated by the moonlight. A strange determination welled up within her. This wasn't just a mystery—it was a story that demanded to be told.

And she knew where she had to go next.
Midnight under the clock tower

Chapter 3

MIDNIGHT AT THE CLOCK TOWER

The town of Colmar was eerily quiet as the clock struck eleven. Camille wrapped her coat tightly around herself, stepping out into the crisp night air. Her apartment was only a short walk from the clock tower, but each step felt heavier, as if she were approaching something far greater than herself.

The letters rested in her bag, their presence a weight she couldn't ignore. The final words of Jules echoed in her mind: "Midnight, my love. There, under its shadow, I shall wait for you."

The clock tower loomed ahead, its imposing silhouette a stark contrast against the star-studded sky. The closer she got, the more her heart raced. She didn't fully understand why she was here. Perhaps it was her writer's curiosity, or maybe it was the inexplicable pull she felt toward Jules and his story.

The square beneath the clock tower was deserted, the shops and cafés shuttered for the night. A lone streetlamp flickered, casting long shadows over the cobblestones. Camille stood beneath the tower, her breath visible in the chilly air.

She glanced at her watch: 11:45 PM. Fifteen minutes until midnight.

As she waited, her thoughts wandered. What was she hoping to find here? Some trace of Jules and Élise? A forgotten relic of their past? Or was this simply an act of

desperation, a way to feel closer to a story that had captured her heart?

The minutes ticked by, the silence broken only by the occasional rustle of leaves. Then, as the clock struck midnight, the air around her shifted. It was subtle at first—a faint chill, a whisper of movement.

"Élise?"

The voice was soft, barely more than a murmur, but it froze Camille in place. She turned slowly, her eyes searching the shadows.

Standing beneath the clock tower was a man. His figure was bathed in moonlight, his features sharp and hauntingly beautiful. He wore a tailored suit that looked as though it belonged to another era, and his dark eyes glimmered with an emotion Camille couldn't name.

Her breath caught. "Jules?" she whispered, the name escaping her lips before she could stop herself.

The man's expression shifted, a mix of hope and disbelief. "Élise, is it really you?"

Camille took a step back, her mind reeling. "I... I'm not Élise," she stammered. "My name is Camille. I found your letters."

His face fell, but the hope in his eyes didn't completely fade. "Camille," he said, testing the name. "You look just like her."

"I found them in an old desk," she said, her voice trembling. "The letters you wrote to Élise. I... I had to know what happened."

Jules studied her, his gaze penetrating. "I've been waiting here," he said finally. "Waiting for her. For over a century."

The weight of his words hit her like a tidal wave. "A century?" she echoed. "That's impossible."

He gave a sad smile. "It should be. But time... it doesn't work the same for me anymore. Not since that night."

"What happened?" Camille asked, her voice barely above a whisper.

Jules' eyes darkened, his expression filled with sorrow. "We were supposed to meet here. Midnight, under the clock tower. But she never came. I waited for hours, days, weeks... And then I learned the truth. Élise was gone."

He paused, his voice breaking. "But something tethered me to this place. Perhaps it was my love for her, or the promise we made. I don't know. All I know is that I've been here ever since, unable to move on."

Camille's heart ached for him. She reached into her bag and pulled out the letters, holding them out to him. "These belong to you."

Jules hesitated before taking them, his fingers brushing against hers. "Thank you," he said softly, his eyes glistening with unshed tears.

As he leafed through the letters, a strange silence enveloped them. Camille felt a connection to this man—this ghost of a love that had endured beyond time.

"Why me?" she asked suddenly. "Why now?"

Jules looked up, his gaze steady. "Because you found them. Because you came."

The clock struck twelve-thirty, the chimes echoing through the empty square. Jules folded the letters carefully, tucking them into his coat.

"Camille," he said, his voice filled with quiet resolve. "There's something about you... something familiar. I don't know why, but I feel as though I've known you before."

Her pulse quickened, a strange unease settling over her. "What do you mean?"

He stepped closer, his presence both comforting and overwhelming. "I think you're here for a reason. Perhaps you were meant to find me. To help me."

"Help you how?"

"To finish what Élise and I couldn't," he said. "To finally let go."

Camille stared at him, her mind racing. She had come here seeking answers, but all she had found were more questions. Who was Jules, truly? And why did she feel as though her own fate was somehow entwined with his?

As the night deepened, Camille realized one thing with certainty: this was only the beginning

Chapter 4
ECHOES OF THE PAST

Camille awoke the next morning with the events of the previous night playing on a loop in her mind. Meeting Jules had felt surreal, like stepping into one of her own unfinished stories. She sat by her window, staring at the clock tower in the distance, its silent presence both comforting and foreboding.

Jules' words haunted her: "To finish what Élise and I couldn't... to finally let go."

She wasn't sure what he meant or why she felt such a powerful connection to his story, but she knew she couldn't walk away now. Jules had waited a century, tethered to this place by love and loss. She owed it to him—and to herself—to uncover the truth.

Later that day, Camille returned to the library, armed with more determination than ever. She approached the elderly librarian, who gave her a knowing smile.

"Back again?" the librarian asked.

"I need to know more about Élise Moreau," Camille said. "The woman who died near the clock tower in 1903. Do you have anything about her?"

The librarian furrowed her brow. "Élise Moreau... let me check." She disappeared behind the counter and returned a few minutes later with a small, worn ledger. "This is an old town registry. It might have some information."

Camille flipped through the pages, her heart pounding. Finally, she found the entry:

Élise Moreau. Born 1881. Died October 12, 1903.

Beside her name was a brief note: "Tragic accident. Survived by fiancé Jules Bernard."

"Fiancé?" Camille murmured, her fingers tracing the faded ink.

The librarian nodded. "Yes, I remember now. It was quite the scandal back then. Élise was from a wealthy family, and Jules... well, he wasn't. Their engagement caused quite a stir. People said their love was doomed from the start."

Camille's chest tightened. The letters had hinted at obstacles, but now she understood the gravity of their situation. Society had stood against them, and fate had been no kinder.

"Do you know anything about Jules?" she asked.

The librarian tilted her head thoughtfully. "Not much. After Élise died, he disappeared. Some say he left town. Others believe he never recovered from her death."

Camille thanked the librarian and left, her mind spinning with possibilities. If Jules had disappeared after Élise's death, how could he still be here?

That evening, Camille returned to the clock tower. The sun was setting, casting a golden glow over the cobblestones. Jules was already there, standing in the shadow of the tower, his gaze distant.

"You came back," he said softly as she approached.

"I need to understand," Camille said. "Why you're still here. Why this happened to you."

Jules turned to her, his expression weary. "I've asked myself the same questions for a century. All I know is that I couldn't move on. Something held me here—my love for Élise, my guilt, or maybe just the promise we made."

"But there's more to it," Camille said. "There has to be." She hesitated before continuing. "I went to the library today. I found records of Élise... and of you. They said you were her fiancé."

Jules' eyes softened. "We were to be married in secret. Her family disapproved, but we didn't care. All we wanted was to be together."

Camille felt a pang of sympathy. "But then she died."

Jules nodded, his voice thick with emotion. "I waited for her that night, beneath this very tower. When she didn't come, I searched everywhere. And then I learned... she was gone. I thought my life ended that night. But instead, I became... this."

Camille stepped closer, her heart breaking for him. "Jules, I think there's a reason I found your letters. Maybe I'm supposed to help you find peace."

He met her gaze, a flicker of hope in his eyes. "How?"
"I don't know yet," she admitted. "But I'll figure it out."

Jules smiled faintly, the first real smile she had seen from him. "Thank you, Camille. You don't know what this means to me."

As the evening deepened, Camille and Jules sat together beneath the clock tower, the town quiet around them. He told her stories of Élise—how they had met at a summer festival, how she had slipped him a note beneath the table when her parents weren't looking, how they had danced under the stars.

"She was fearless," Jules said, his voice filled with reverence.

"She made me believe we could conquer anything. Even time."

Camille listened, captivated by his words. But as he spoke, a strange feeling settled over her—a sense of déjà vu, as though she had heard these stories before.

"Jules," she said hesitantly, "do you believe in reincarnation?"

He frowned slightly. "I'm not sure. Why?"

She hesitated, unsure how to explain the pull she felt toward him, the way his story resonated with her on a level she couldn't explain. "I don't know. It's just... sometimes I feel like I know you. Like I've always known you."

Jules studied her, his gaze searching. "Perhaps you do," he said quietly. "Perhaps there's more to this than either of us understands."

As the clock struck ten, Camille stood reluctantly. "I should go," she said.

Jules rose with her, his expression unreadable. "Thank you, Camille. For listening. For caring."

She nodded, a lump forming in her throat. "I'll be back tomorrow. We'll figure this out together."

As she walked away, the feeling of déjà vu lingered, stronger than ever. Something about Jules, about this story, felt deeply familiar—as though she had lived it before.

And deep down, she couldn't shake the feeling that she and Élise were connected in ways she had yet to understand.

Chapter 5
UNRAVELLING THE THREADS

The days that followed were filled with quiet contemplation and restless nights. Camille couldn't stop thinking about Jules, about the letters, and about the strange connection she felt to Élise. Her life had always been cantered around words, around creating stories that blurred the lines between reality and fiction. But this—this was something different. Something too real to ignore.

It was a crisp morning when she received a letter at her doorstep. There was no return address, only her name scrawled in familiar handwriting—Jules's handwriting. Her heart raced as she tore it open.

My Dearest Camille,

The days since you've arrived have been both a comfort and a torment. I cannot shake the feeling that fate has brought you to me. Perhaps you are the key to finally setting me free, or perhaps we are two lost souls caught in a cycle of love and loss that neither of us can escape.

I have been to the place where Élise and I planned our future. The park by the river, where we were to marry in secret. I will meet you there tonight, at dusk, when the sky turns gold.

Perhaps there, in the place where we once dreamed of forever, we will find the answers.

Yours,
Jules

Camille felt a strange thrill, a sense of urgency she couldn't explain. She had to go. There was something in Jules's words, a pull, a promise that she couldn't ignore. She wasn't sure what awaited her at the park by the river, but she knew she had to follow the thread he had thrown to her.

That evening, Camille found herself standing at the entrance to the park. The sky was painted with hues of orange and purple, the river glistening beneath the fading light. The park seemed like a dream—a place suspended in time, much like the love story Jules had shared with Élise.

She walked deeper into the park, her footsteps muffled by the soft earth beneath her shoes. The trees loomed overhead, their branches twisting and reaching toward the sky. In the distance, she could see Jules standing by the riverbank, his back to her.

He turned as she approached, his expression a mixture of relief and something else—something that made her heart ache.

"You came," he said, his voice hoarse. "I didn't know if you would."

"I couldn't stay away," Camille replied, her voice barely above a whisper.

Jules stepped toward her, his gaze intense. "I've been thinking a lot about what you said—about reincarnation. About how you feel like you know me, like you've always known me." He paused, as if gathering his thoughts. "I don't know if I believe in it, but there's something about you, Camille. Something that feels... familiar. Like we've crossed paths before."

Camille felt her breath catch in her throat. The same sensation she had experienced the night she first met him

returned, stronger than ever. The strange pull, the sense that her destiny was tied to this man in a way she couldn't explain.

"I don't know what it is," she admitted, her voice trembling. "But I feel it too. And it scares me."

Jules took a step closer, his hand reaching for hers. "Maybe we're meant to uncover the truth together. Maybe we're meant to break the cycle."

The air between them seemed to crackle with tension. Camille's pulse quickened, her mind racing. She had come here looking for answers, but what if the answers she found only deepened the mystery?

"What if we can't break it?" she whispered. "What if this is all there is? A love that can never be?"

Jules's eyes softened, his expression filled with both sadness and hope. "Then we will make the most of the time we have. Even if it's just for a moment."

Camille's heart ached at his words. She wanted to believe him. She wanted to believe that somehow, despite the centuries that separated them, they could find a way to be together. But there was so much she didn't understand. So many pieces that didn't fit.

"I need to know more about Élise," she said, pulling her hand away gently. "I need to understand everything—the letters, the accident, why she never showed up."

Jules nodded, his gaze distant. "I've told you all I know. The rest is lost to time."

"Maybe it's not," Camille said, her voice firm. "Maybe we can find the answers. Together."

Jules stared at her for a long moment, his eyes filled with a mixture of longing and fear. "I want that too," he said softly. "But I don't know if I'm ready to face the truth."

The silence between them stretched, heavy and suffocating. Camille could feel the weight of the centuries pressing down on them both. The love, the loss, the unfulfilled promises. And the lingering question: Could they truly find peace, or were they forever doomed to relive the past?

"I think I know where to look," Camille said suddenly,

Chapter 6
THE SECRETS BENEATH THE STONE

The church on the outskirts of Colmar was old, its stone walls weathered by time and history. Camille had always been drawn to it as a child, her grandmother often telling her stories of the sacred space where secrets were kept and souls were laid to rest. Now, as an adult, Camille felt a deep sense of purpose as she stood before the weathered wooden doors, which creaked open as if acknowledging her arrival.

Jules was beside her, his gaze scanning the church grounds. He seemed almost hesitant, as though the place held memories he wasn't ready to confront.

"Are you sure about this?" he asked softly. "What if the truth is worse than we imagine?"

Camille turned to him, her resolve unwavering. "I have to know, Jules. For both our sakes. We can't keep living in the shadows of the past."

Jules nodded, but there was a lingering sadness in his eyes. He had been waiting for so long, and Camille could feel the weight of his uncertainty, the fear that the truth might finally shatter whatever fragile hope he still clung to.

Inside, the church was dimly lit, with stained-glass windows casting colourful patterns on the stone floors. The air smelled of aged wood and incense, the silence broken only by the distant echo of footsteps. Camille's heart raced as she

walked toward the back of the church, where an old wooden door stood ajar, leading to the archives.

Jules hesitated at the threshold, his eyes flicking between Camille and the darkness beyond. "I've never been here... not since... well, not since that night."

Camille reached out, placing a gentle hand on his arm. "You don't have to come if you don't want to," she said softly, her voice filled with understanding.

But Jules shook his head. "No. If we're going to do this, we do it together."

The archives were lined with dusty shelves, filled with old scrolls, books, and leather-bound journals. Camille's eyes scanned the titles, her fingers tracing the spines of the books as she moved deeper into the room. She knew the records they were looking for—anything that might shed light on Élise's death, on the love that had been torn apart so cruelly.

Jules walked slowly, his steps heavy. He was not ready for what they might uncover, but the desire to know the truth was stronger than his fear.

Camille reached a shelf at the far end of the room and pulled out a heavy ledger, its leather cover cracked and worn. She blew the dust off the cover and opened it to the first page, her eyes skimming the words.

"The Marriage Records of Colmar. 1903."

Her breath hitched. This was it. The moment that might hold the answers she had been searching for. She flipped to the section marked "Deaths" and scanned the names, her heart pounding in her chest. And then she found it.

Élise Moreau. Died October 12, 1903.

The words were simple, but the note beside it was what made Camille's heart stop.

"Cause of death: Accidental drowning in the river. Body discovered at dawn. No foul play suspected."

Jules stepped forward, his voice a whisper. "The river…"

Camille nodded, her mind racing. "She drowned... but why was she by the river that night? Why didn't she meet you under the clock tower?"

Jules closed his eyes, pain flooding his features. "We had planned to run away together. We were going to meet in secret by the river. But she never came."

Camille paused, absorbing the weight of the revelation. If Élise had drowned on the night of their meeting, it meant that Jules's wait had been in vain. The tragedy was more profound than she had imagined. She had always known that Élise's death had been sudden, but to learn of its nature—it shook her.

She continued reading the ledger, hoping for more information, when her eyes caught another entry further down. It was a note written in a different hand, as if someone had added it after the fact.

"Jules Bernard. Body never found. Vanished after the death of Élise. Presumed dead."

Camille's stomach dropped. Jules's disappearance had been more mysterious than she'd realized. It wasn't just that he had left town after Élise's death; he had vanished completely, leaving behind nothing but rumors and unanswered questions.

Jules's voice, low and strained, broke through her thoughts. "I never... I didn't mean to disappear. I couldn't

bear the thought of living without her. So, I..." He trailed off, as if the words were too painful to continue.

Camille's heart went out to him. He had been trapped in time, consumed by grief. But now, standing in the dimly lit archives, she saw something new in him—a man who had been lost to himself for far too long, searching for a way back to the love he had lost.

"Jules," Camille whispered, her voice thick with emotion. "This—this was never just about Élise. You've been stuck in this place, in this time, because you couldn't let go. You couldn't move forward."

Jules looked at her, his eyes filled with unshed tears. "I couldn't. And I didn't know how to."

Camille placed the ledger down gently, her fingers trembling. She knew now, without a doubt, that the reason Jules was still here, waiting for Élise, was because he had never truly let go of the love they had shared. But that didn't mean he had to remain stuck in the past forever.

"We can't change the past," Camille said softly, "but we can honour it. And maybe... maybe that will help you find peace."

Jules stared at her for a long time, his expression unreadable. And then, for the first time since Camille had met him, he smiled—a faint, bittersweet smile, full of both sorrow and acceptance.

"Perhaps," he said, his voice hoarse but steady. "Perhaps it's time to finally let go."

As they left the church that evening, Camille felt the weight of their discovery settle over them both. The past had been revealed in all its heart-wrenching truth. But the future

was still unknown, still filled with possibilities. She had helped Jules uncover the truth about Élise's death, but she knew there was still so much left to understand—about their connection, about the mysterious force that had brought them together, and about whether they could break the cycle of love and loss that had bound them.

But for now, as the sun dipped below the horizon and the cool evening air wrapped around them, Camille felt a sense of peace that had eluded her since the moment she first opened the desk drawer. The answers were out there, and she was ready to continue the journey—to unravel the final threads of this timeless love story.

Chapter 7
The Clock Tower's Secret

The night was colder than usual, a sharp chill in the air that seemed to match the weight of everything Camille had learned in the last few days. As she and Jules walked through the cobbled streets of Colmar, the echoes of their footsteps seemed to reverberate through the quiet town, as if the city itself was holding its breath.

Jules hadn't spoken much since they left the church, his thoughts clearly preoccupied. Camille could sense the heaviness in him, the burden of a century's worth of grief and longing. But she knew that this—this was a turning point. The truth had been uncovered, and now it was time to face the final piece of the puzzle: the clock tower.

"I haven't been back here since..." Jules began, his voice barely a whisper. He glanced toward the tower, its silhouette standing tall against the moonlit sky. "Since the night Élise was supposed to meet me."

Camille didn't need to ask for more details. She could see it in his eyes—the weight of a memory that had lived inside him for a hundred years. A memory of waiting, of hoping, of believing against all odds that Élise would appear and their love would be rekindled. But that hope had turned into an endless cycle of despair, and it was only now, with Camille at his side, that he was beginning to see the possibility of breaking free.

"I don't know if I'm ready to face it," Jules admitted, his voice trembling. "What if it's too much?"

Camille stopped walking and turned to him. "We've already faced so much together, Jules. We've uncovered the truth, and now we have to finish what we started. We can't keep living in the shadows of the past. You have to let go."

He nodded, his expression softening. "I know. But it's not that simple."

Together, they reached the base of the clock tower, its old stone steps winding up into the night. Camille could feel the history in the air—the weight of all the years that had passed, the promises made and broken beneath this very tower.

"It's time," she said, her voice steady despite the uncertainty that churned inside her. "We're here to break the cycle. Together."

Jules hesitated but took a deep breath before starting up the steps, Camille close behind him. The climb was slow, each step a reminder of the years that had passed since that fateful night, but also of how far they had come. When they reached the top, the view of Colmar was breath taking—its rooftops bathed in the soft glow of the moon, the streets empty and still.

At the centre of the tower was the great clock, its hands frozen at midnight—the very hour when Élise had been meant to arrive. Jules stood before it, his gaze fixed on the clock, his face a mixture of longing and sorrow.

"This is where it all ended," he said quietly. "This is where I've been waiting all these years."

Camille stepped closer, her heart heavy with understanding. She had come to know Jules so well in these past days—his pain, his need for closure, and his fear of

moving on. But now, as they stood together in this timeless place, Camille felt the weight of their love story—a love that had transcended time but had also been held prisoner by it.

She reached out, gently placing a hand on his arm. "Jules, you've been waiting for a hundred years. But Élise is gone. The truth is, she never made it here. We can't change the past. We can't bring her back."

He turned to her, his eyes filled with a raw emotion that spoke volumes. "I know. But I couldn't stop myself from believing that somehow, we could be together again."

Camille swallowed the lump in her throat. She had known from the moment she had discovered the letters that this was going to be a difficult journey. But now, standing here with him, she realized just how much Jules had sacrificed for a love that had never had the chance to blossom.

"I think..." Camille began, her voice steady but filled with tenderness, "I think it's time for you to finally let her go. To find peace. You deserve that, Jules. You don't have to carry this burden anymore."

Jules closed his eyes, his face taut with the weight of his memories. For a long moment, he said nothing. The only sound was the wind whispering through the cracks of the tower, the ticking of the clock as if it were counting down to something.

"I don't know how to let go," he finally whispered.

Camille stepped closer, her hand finding his. "You don't have to do it alone. I'm here, Jules. I've always been here, even before we met."

Jules looked at her, his eyes searching hers as if looking for something—a sign, a truth, anything that would show him

that it was finally time to move on. And then, with a deep sigh, he nodded.

"I've been holding on for so long," he said softly. "But I can't keep living like this."

Camille smiled gently, her thumb brushing over the back of his hand. "You don't have to. It's time to step into the light, Jules. Time to break free."

Together, they stood in the quiet of the tower, watching the clock's hands begin to move again, slowly at first, but gaining momentum. The world around them seemed to shift as if the universe itself was acknowledging the end of an era.

For a moment, everything felt still, as if time itself had paused to honour the love that had existed between Jules and Élise—and the love that had bloomed between Camille and Jules. In this moment, there was no past, no future, only the present.

And in that present, they were free.

The hands of the clock moved forward, and as the first light of dawn touched the horizon, Camille knew that Jules was finally at peace. The endless cycle of waiting, of longing, had come to an end.

But as they descended the tower, their hands still intertwined, Camille couldn't shake the feeling that this wasn't the end of their story. There was something more—something that transcended even time itself.

And she was ready to discover what that was

Chapter 8

THE AWAKENING OF LOVE

The days that followed felt like a dream. Colmar seemed to shift in subtle ways, as if the town itself was letting out a long-held breath, the weight of its history finally lifting. Camille and Jules moved through the streets together, side by side, no longer bound by the past but by the shared understanding they had forged. The sense of liberation that had come after breaking the cycle was palpable, and yet, Camille couldn't shake the feeling that there was still something unfinished—something they hadn't yet uncovered.

It had been a week since they had stood beneath the clock tower, and yet, every morning Camille woke with a lingering sense of wonder, as if the universe were speaking to her in ways she could barely comprehend. Her connection to Jules had deepened, not just in the way they had shared their pasts, but in a profound, almost unexplainable sense. It felt as though the fabric of time itself had stretched and pulled to bring them together, to create a new chapter in a story that had long been written in the stars.

One evening, as they sat at a small café by the canal, Camille watched the reflections of the old town buildings dance in the water, the soft hum of the evening settling around them. Jules had been quieter than usual, his expression distant as if lost in thought.

"You've been quiet," Camille remarked, her voice gentle. "What's on your mind?"

Jules took a deep breath, his gaze drifting to the rippling water. "I've been thinking a lot. About what comes next."

Camille frowned slightly. "What do you mean?"

He turned to face her, his expression serious. "For so long, I've been trapped in the past, waiting for something that was never going to happen. But now, everything is different. I'm free. But I'm also... uncertain. What does this freedom mean, Camille?"

Camille felt a pang of understanding. Jules had spent so long carrying the weight of Élise's memory that it was no wonder he didn't know what to do with the freedom that had been given to him. He had been lost in the space between life and death for so long that now, with his past finally at rest, he had to find his own place in the world.

"I think..." Camille began, her heart full of empathy, "I think freedom is about embracing the present. It's about letting go of what you thought your destiny was and opening yourself up to new possibilities."

Jules nodded slowly, his eyes softening. "You're right. I can feel it—this overwhelming sense that life is... still waiting for me, for us. But I don't know how to begin."

A silence settled between them, comfortable but filled with unspoken words. Camille reached across the table, taking his hand in hers. The touch was warm, grounding them both in the present.

"We don't have to have all the answers right now," Camille said softly. "We've already come so far. Maybe the next step is just taking it one day at a time."

Jules squeezed her hand, his gaze searching hers. "One day at a time," he repeated, as if testing the phrase, trying to understand it in a way that felt real to him.

And then, a small smile tugged at the corners of his lips, a smile that seemed to carry the weight of a hundred years of waiting, and the sweetness of finally being able to let go. "I think I can do that."

Over the next few days, Camille and Jules began to rebuild their lives together. They explored Colmar in a way that felt new and exhilarating. They spent hours wandering through the town's flower-lined streets, laughing at little things, savouring the quiet moments that came with the simplicity of being present. There was no rushing, no pressure to figure everything out all at once. They were two people discovering each other for the first time, not as echoes of a past love, but as two souls intertwined in the here and now.

But it wasn't just Colmar that felt different—it was the world itself. With each passing day, Camille felt a deeper connection to her own life, her own dreams. She had spent so much time searching for answers, for the truth about Élise and Jules that she had forgotten to look inward, to question her own place in this story. But now, with Jules by her side, something inside her began to shift.

She began to write again, her fingers dancing across the pages of her journal, not with the urgency of finding an answer, but with the peace that came from embracing the unknown. She wrote of the town, of the canals, of the quiet love that had bloomed between her and Jules. But she also wrote about herself—about her fears, her hopes, and the strange, inexplicable force that had brought her to this moment.

One evening, as they sat by the canal watching the sunset, Camille turned to Jules, a thought forming in her mind.

"You know," she said, her voice thoughtful, "I've been thinking about those letters we found—the ones from Jules to Élise. I can't help but wonder... what would have happened if

they had met that night? Would their love have been enough to change the course of history?"

Jules looked at her, his eyes searching, and for a moment, she thought she saw a glimmer of something new—something that wasn't bound by the past.

"I think," he said slowly, "that love is powerful, Camille. But sometimes, it's not enough to change the course of things. Sometimes, it just needs to exist, to be real, even if only for a moment."

Camille's heart swelled at his words. She realized then that love, in all its forms, wasn't about perfection or time—it was about connection, about the moments that shaped us and the choices we made because of them.

"Maybe," she said, her voice barely above a whisper, "that's all we really need."

They sat in silence for a while, watching the last of the sun's rays disappear behind the town's skyline. And for the first time since Camille had stumbled upon those letters, she felt a profound sense of peace—a peace that came from knowing that some loves were meant to be fleeting, others were meant to last, and some... some would transcend time itself.

In that moment, as the world around them faded into twilight, Camille knew that her journey with Jules wasn't just about rewriting history. It was about creating a new story—one that was entirely their own.

And as they stood up to walk together into the evening, side by side, Camille felt an unspoken promise settle in her heart. No matter what the future held, they would face it together.

Chapter 9
The Echoes of Tomorrow

The days grew longer, the warm embrace of spring beginning to settle over Colmar. The once-crisp air was now soft with the scent of blooming flowers, and the town felt alive in ways it hadn't before—perhaps because Camille and Jules had, in some quiet, profound way, begun to live fully in the present. They no longer lingered in the shadows of the past, but embraced the uncertainty of the future with open hearts.

But despite their growing connection, there was still something lingering in Camille's heart—a quiet question she couldn't quite silence. The feeling of being pulled toward something she didn't fully understand. Something beyond the love she shared with Jules. It was as if the threads of fate, the very forces that had brought them together, were hinting at a deeper truth she was yet to discover.

It was late one evening when Camille sat down to write in her journal, the candlelight flickering softly on the table beside her. She had been working on a new story—one that felt more personal, more real. It was about love, of course, but it was also about the layers of time and memory that shaped who people were, even if they couldn't see it. As she wrote, her thoughts drifted back to the letters, to Élise, and to the deep, eternal connection she now shared with Jules.

But as she wrote, a thought struck her—one that hadn't fully occurred to her until now.

What if all of this was more than just a love story? What if it was something else entirely?

She stopped, her pen hovering over the page as the words came to her: Élise was me.

The realization hit her like a wave, crashing over her, sweeping away the confusion that had clouded her mind for days. She wasn't just an observer of this love story, she wasn't just Camille, a writer lost in the past. She had always been Élise. Not in the literal sense—no, that wasn't it. But in a way that defied reason and logic, her soul had always belonged to this love story.

The more she thought about it, the clearer it became. The pull toward the antique desk, the letters that had found her as if guided by an invisible hand, the undeniable sense of déjà vu whenever she was near Jules—it wasn't just coincidence. She had been drawn to this place, to this time, because it was where she belonged.

The realization left her breathless. It was as if the veil between past and present had lifted, and she could see the intricate web that had connected her to Jules for lifetimes.

But with the realization came a wave of fear. If she was Élise, if she had lived this story before, what did that mean for her future with Jules? Could she continue to walk this path with him, knowing that it was destined to repeat? Or was she doomed to be trapped in this cycle of love and loss?

Her thoughts were interrupted by a soft knock at the door. She blinked, the world around her coming back into focus. She stood, her legs shaky, as she crossed the room to open it.

Jules stood on the other side, his face illuminated by the soft light of the hallway. His eyes were searching, as if he could sense something was amiss.

"Camille," he said gently, "are you okay?"

She nodded, her heart racing in her chest. "I... I think I just realized something."

He stepped closer, his gaze intense. "What?"

She hesitated, the words heavy on her tongue. "I think I'm Élise. In some way... I think I've always been."

Jules's expression softened, as if the weight of her words were sinking in. "What do you mean?"

"I've been thinking about everything—the letters, our connection, the way I've been pulled to this place. To you. It's not just a coincidence, Jules. It's like... like I've always known you, always loved you. Even when we didn't know it."

Jules was silent for a long moment, his brow furrowed in thought. Camille held her breath, unsure of what he would say. Would he understand? Would he believe her?

Finally, he spoke, his voice calm but filled with emotion. "I don't know if I fully understand it, Camille. But I've always felt something with you. Something that goes beyond logic or reason. It's like—like we were meant to find each other, even if we didn't know why."

A tear slipped down Camille's cheek, though she couldn't quite say why. "It's all so overwhelming," she whispered. "What if we're just meant to repeat the same mistakes? What if we can't change anything? What if I can't let go of Élise's past?"

Jules gently cupped her face in his hands, his touch grounding her. "Camille, we can't control the past. But we have the power to choose what happens next. We can choose to create something new together."

She looked up at him, her heart swelling with love and uncertainty in equal measure. "But what if this love isn't enough? What if it can't change the course of history?"

Jules smiled softly, his thumb brushing away the tear on her cheek. "Maybe love isn't about changing everything. Maybe it's about finding the courage to live in the present, to love without fear of what comes next."

The weight of his words settled into her chest, and for the first time, she felt a sense of peace wash over her. She wasn't trapped in a cycle. She wasn't Élise reliving the same life. She was Camille, and she had the power to shape her own destiny.

"I love you, Jules," she said, her voice steady. "And I'm not afraid anymore."

"I love you too, Camille," he whispered, his lips meeting hers in a soft kiss, the world outside fading into nothingness as they embraced their future, together.

The next morning, Camille woke to the soft light of dawn streaming through her window. She felt different, lighter, as if a weight had been lifted from her chest. The past was no longer a shadow hanging over her; it was simply a part of the story that had brought her to this moment.

She walked to the window, gazing out at the town she had come to love. Colmar, with its winding streets and peaceful canals, had become a symbol of her journey—not just through time, but through the complexities of the heart.

She had loved, lost, and learned. But now, for the first time, Camille was ready to step into the future. The echoes of the past no longer held her captive. It was time to create something new, to live a life filled with possibility, with love that transcended time but wasn't bound by it.

And as she looked out over the town, she knew that this was just the beginning of their story. A story of love that would last, not through the constraints of time, but through the strength of their hearts.

The future was hers. It was theirs. And together, they would write the next chapter

Chapter 10
THE FINAL LETTER

The morning after her quiet moment of realization, Camille stood before the antique desk in her apartment, her fingers brushing the edges of the weathered wood. The desk had once been a symbol of the past—a relic of someone else's love story—but now it felt like part of her own journey. It had brought her to Jules, to Élise's forgotten promises, and to a future she was finally beginning to shape on her own terms.

But something tugged at her. A feeling deep within her that there was more to the story. There had to be something else hidden in this mystery, a piece of the puzzle still missing. The letters had been a bridge between her past and her present, and now, she wondered if they held the final answer.

She sat down at the desk, her heart pounding in anticipation, and opened the drawer where the letters had first been discovered. She had read them all—those beautiful, heart-wrenching words. But this time, something was different. This time, she could sense the presence of the missing letter.

Her eyes scanned the contents of the drawer, and there, wedged beneath the pile of yellowed papers, she saw it. A single envelope, sealed with wax. She had never noticed it before. The handwriting on the front was elegant but hurried—an unmistakable hand that felt familiar in a way she couldn't explain.

It was addressed simply: To Camille.

Her breath caught in her throat. She hesitated only for a moment before tearing open the envelope, her hands trembling.

Inside was a single sheet of paper, the ink still fresh despite its age.

My Dearest Camille,

By the time you read this, you will know everything—know that I was never truly lost to time. That I had always been waiting for you, even before you knew it. The love we shared, the love you will come to know, is eternal. It transcends every barrier—every wall between worlds and lifetimes.

I have watched you grow, Camille, and with each step, you have come closer to the truth. You are Élise, but more than that, you are both the past and the future, the love of a thousand lifetimes bound by a thread of fate that no force can sever. But now, the time has come for you to choose—truly choose. Choose whether you will let go of the past, or allow it to consume you forever.

Know that I have waited for you longer than words can convey. My heart, tethered to this town and to you, will never be free until you make your decision. And, in this final letter, I give you one last gift: the chance to free both of us from the cycle that has bound us together for so long. But you must decide. Not as Élise, not as Camille—but as yourself.

I love you, now and forever.
Jules.

Camille sat back, stunned, the letter slipping from her hands and falling gently onto the desk. A thousand emotions swirled within her—love, confusion, fear, and relief. Jules had known. He had known who she truly was before she had even discovered it herself. He had waited for her, not just in this life but in every life before. And now, it was up to her to make the final choice.

She thought of the promise she had made—to live fully, without fear of what came next. She thought of the love they had shared, of the fleeting moments in the town of Colmar that had felt timeless. It was beautiful, yes. But she was not ready to be trapped in the past forever. Not as Élise. Not as anyone other than herself.

The weight of the decision settled into her bones. She could choose to let go of the cycle—break the chain of love that had spanned centuries. She could choose freedom, the freedom to live fully in the present with Jules, and embrace a future without the ghosts of the past haunting them.

But what would that future look like? Could she truly let go of a love that had followed her through time? Could she walk away from the love that had, in many ways, defined who she was?

Her thoughts turned to Jules. She had never known a love like this, and though the past was filled with heartache, the present was filled with possibility. He had always been there for her—patient, understanding, loving her through every moment of uncertainty. Could she truly turn her back on him?

As the sun dipped low, casting a golden glow across the cobblestones outside, Camille made her decision. She knew, deep in her heart, that the only way forward was to embrace the present. To embrace who she was now, and to build the life she wanted—not bound by the constraints of the past, but free to choose her own path.

She stood up, folding the letter carefully and tucking it into her pocket. It was time to find Jules.

As Camille walked through the town toward the old clock tower, she felt the weight of her decision settle on her shoulders. The air was crisp, and the town felt alive with the

hum of spring. The sky was painted in hues of pink and orange as the day began to fade into evening.

When she arrived at the clock tower, she saw Jules standing at the base, waiting for her. His eyes were filled with the same quiet love and hope that had drawn her to him from the very beginning. She could see the question in his gaze—the uncertainty that had lingered ever since their first meeting.

Without a word, Camille crossed the cobblestones and stood before him. She reached for his hand, her fingers trembling slightly as they intertwined with his.

"I've made my decision," she said softly. "I'm not Élise. I'm Camille. And I'm not afraid to live for us, right here, right now."

Jules's eyes searched hers, and for a moment, it was as if the world had stopped. The weight of their shared history, the love that had spanned across lifetimes, seemed to dissipate in that one moment of clarity.

"I love you, Camille," he whispered.
"I love you, too," she replied, her voice steady and strong.

They stood together beneath the clock tower, the hands of time ticking softly above them. The past had taught them everything they needed to know about love and loss, but now it was time to move forward. Together. No more promises to keep. No more ghosts to haunt them.

It was their time.

And in that moment, the world felt perfectly still, as if all of time had finally aligned to grant them the one thing they had always longed for: the chance to live in the present

Chapter 11

BEYOND THE CLOCK

The days that followed Camille's decision were a blur of moments—small, intimate exchanges with Jules that slowly built a new life from the foundation of their shared past. No longer bound by the echoes of a love lost in time, they began to craft a future together. It was simple, beautiful, and entirely their own.

In the mornings, they wandered the streets of Colmar, the town that had become both a witness to their love story and the backdrop of Camille's discovery. The cobblestone streets, the meandering canals, and the charming, ivy-clad houses seemed to wrap around them in a comforting embrace, as if the town itself were protecting them from the world outside. They would stop at the local café, where Jules would order the same coffee, and Camille would laugh as she watched him fumble with the menu, pretending he didn't know exactly what to order.

But their peaceful days were not without their moments of reflection. Jules still carried the weight of a love that had been deferred for so long. He often found himself gazing at the old clock tower, his thoughts drifting to the past, to Élise, to the time that had slipped away. It was a heavy burden that he carried quietly, but Camille knew the way his gaze would soften when he spoke of her. She understood the ache in his heart.

One afternoon, as the sun began to set, casting a warm glow over the town, they found themselves sitting by the canal, watching the boats drift lazily by. Jules turned to Camille, his expression serious.

"I've been thinking a lot about what you said that night—the choice to live for us," he began, his voice low. "And I want you to know that I don't regret it. Not a single moment. But I still carry a part of Élise inside me, and I don't want that to be a burden for you."

Camille reached out and took his hand, squeezing it gently. She could feel the unease in his words, the lingering connection to the past that he had yet to fully sever. He had loved Élise deeply, and that love had shaped him in ways Camille couldn't fully understand.

"I know you do, Jules," she replied softly. "And I would never ask you to forget her. But you don't need to carry that weight alone. We're building something new. A love that is ours—something that belongs only to us."

Jules looked at her, his eyes searching hers for something. For reassurance, for understanding. And in that moment, Camille realized that what they were building was not just a future together—it was a way to reconcile the past with the present, to find peace in the spaces between times.

"I've waited for so long," he murmured. "And now, I just want to be here. With you."

Camille smiled, leaning in to kiss him gently. The world around them seemed to pause, as if holding its breath in reverence of their quiet connection. The boats continued to drift by, the soft hum of the town blending with the distant chirping of crickets. It was a moment of pure peace, the kind that came when two souls finally found each other after years of searching.

As the days passed, Camille and Jules began to explore their relationship in new ways. They spent hours talking about their hopes, their dreams, and their fears. They shared stories of their childhoods, their loves, and their losses. Camille told

him about her struggles as a writer, about the novels she had abandoned, and the words that had yet to find their home. Jules spoke of his years of waiting—how he had wandered through life, unable to fully connect with anyone, always searching for something he couldn't name until he met her.

They visited the old clock tower one last time, not to relive the past, but to say goodbye to the promise of an unfulfilled love. Together, they stood beneath its shadow, holding hands, the sound of the ticking clock marking the passage of time as they let go of the weight of history.

"I think it's time we let it go," Camille whispered, her voice full of certainty.

Jules nodded, his fingers tightening around hers. "Yes. Time to move forward."

They stood there for a moment, breathing in the air of the town that had witnessed their journey—a journey that had transcended the boundaries of time, a journey that had led them back to each other.

Weeks turned into months, and Camille and Jules continued to build their life together. The town of Colmar remained their sanctuary, a place where they could escape from the world and just be. But even in their quiet moments, Camille couldn't help but feel a strange sense of completion. The past had been laid to rest, and now, the present was all that mattered.

One evening, as they walked hand in hand along the canal, Jules stopped and pulled her gently into his arms. "Camille, I don't think I ever really understood what it meant to live until I met you."

She smiled, brushing a stray lock of hair from his forehead. "I feel the same way. I spent so much time running

from my past, but now I understand that it's the moments like this—right now—that matter."

Jules kissed her softly, his lips lingering as if savouring the sweetness of the present. "Then let's make every moment count. Together."

And so they did. With each passing day, they created a love that was entirely their own—a love not defined by time, but by the choices they made in the here and now.

For Camille and Jules, the clock no longer held power over them. They were no longer bound by the promises of the past or the fear of the future. They had finally discovered the one truth that had eluded them for so long: that love, in its truest form, exists beyond the confines of time.

And as they walked through the streets of Colmar, hand in hand, the world felt infinitely larger, and yet, perfectly small.

Chapter 12
A New Beginning

The sun had risen early that day, casting a soft golden light over the town of Colmar. Camille stood at the window of their small apartment, watching the mist begin to lift from the cobblestone streets below. It had been months since she and Jules had decided to leave the past behind and build a life together, and yet, each day felt like the first—a new beginning, a new chapter in a love story that had been centuries in the making.

Her fingers brushed the edge of a fresh manuscript that lay on the desk—a novel she had begun writing after her discovery of the antique desk and its letters. It was no longer about Élise and Jules. It was no longer about recreating a love that had been lost. It was about her, Camille, and the stories she had always longed to tell. The characters in her novel now carried a piece of her soul, a reflection of the woman she had become since that fateful day at the clock tower.

Jules entered the room, his footsteps light against the wooden floor. He walked over to her, wrapping his arms around her from behind, his chin resting on her shoulder. "Good morning," he murmured, his voice warm and comforting.

"Good morning," Camille replied, turning in his arms to face him. She smiled up at him, feeling a deep sense of peace settle over her. They had come so far, together, and every day, she found herself more grateful for the love they shared. The weight of the past had finally been lifted, and the future stretched before them like a canvas, waiting to be painted with new memories.

Jules looked down at the manuscript on the desk, his brow furrowing slightly. "How's the writing going?"

Camille smiled softly, her fingers grazing the pages. "It's going well. I've been inspired by everything we've been through. This story isn't just about a love that has endured through time; it's about letting go of the past and embracing the future. It's about finding peace in the present."

Jules kissed the top of her head. "I think that's what we've done, isn't it? We've found peace in each other, in this moment."

Camille nodded, feeling the truth of his words in her heart. "Yes, we have."

Their mornings were often spent like this—quiet, shared moments that spoke louder than any words could. Jules would make coffee while Camille would read or write, and they would sit together, exchanging small glances and occasional laughter, lost in the simplicity of their love. The ordinary, everyday moments that had once seemed so insignificant were now the most precious of all.

But even in the calm of their daily routine, Camille could sense that a new chapter was beginning to unfold. The town of Colmar, which had been a silent witness to their journey, now seemed to pulse with new energy. There was something in the air—something that told her their story was far from over. In fact, it was only just beginning.

Later that afternoon, Camille and Jules decided to take a walk through the town. They strolled hand in hand through the streets, past the rows of colourful houses, the flower stalls, and the small cafes where the locals gathered. Colmar had become more than just the backdrop of their love story; it had become a place of healing, a place where both of them could start fresh.

They stopped by the canal, sitting on a bench overlooking the water, the gentle lapping of the waves soothing in its rhythmic sound. Camille leaned back, her head resting on Jules's shoulder, feeling the warmth of the sun on her skin. She was content—truly content, in a way she had never known before. The love she had with Jules was no longer a shadow of the past, but a vibrant, living thing that grew stronger with every passing day.

"Do you ever think about what might have been?" Jules asked quietly, his voice carrying a hint of uncertainty.

Camille turned her head to look at him, her eyes searching his face. She knew what he was asking. He was wondering if she ever regretted their decision to move forward—to let go of the past and embrace the present, even if it meant leaving behind the memory of Élise and the promise they had made long ago.

"I used to," she said softly, her voice filled with understanding. "I used to wonder if we were making the right choice. But now, when I look at you, when I feel this love between us, I know we made the right decision."

Jules smiled, his eyes filled with a tenderness that made Camille's heart swell. "I'm glad. Because I can't imagine my life without you in it."

"I can't imagine mine without you, either."

They sat in silence for a while, simply enjoying the peace of the moment. The world around them continued to turn, the seasons slowly changing, but in that space, time seemed to stand still. It was as if the past, with all its pain and longing, had faded into the background, and only the present remained—a present filled with love, hope, and the promise of a future yet to be written.

As the days passed, Camille's novel began to take shape, and with each word she wrote, she felt a deeper connection to the story. It was no longer just a way to process her past or to understand the love between Élise and Jules; it was her way of reclaiming her own voice, her own identity. She had found the courage to step into the future, to write her own story, and to live it fully, without the shadows of the past clouding her vision.

One evening, after a long day of writing, Camille sat at the desk, staring at the manuscript before her. The words flowed effortlessly now, each sentence carrying the weight of her experiences, her love for Jules, and the life they were building together. She was no longer trapped in a cycle of regret or longing. She was free—free to love, free to write, free to be herself.

Jules entered the room and leaned against the doorframe, watching her with a quiet smile. "How's the book coming along?"

Camille looked up, her heart swelling with love. "It's coming along beautifully. I think it might be the best thing I've ever written."

Jules stepped forward and placed a kiss on her forehead. "I'm proud of you."

Camille's eyes sparkled with gratitude. "I couldn't have done it without you."

And in that moment, Camille knew that this was just the beginning. The future they were creating together, the life they had built, was only the first of many chapters. They had found something timeless—not in the letters of the past, not in the memories of what could have been—but in the present, in the love they shared, and in the possibility of all the days to come.

With Jules by her side, Camille knew that whatever came next, they would face it together. And that was enough.

As the night fell and the stars began to twinkle above, Camille closed her laptop and took a deep breath. She could hear Jules in the next room, humming softly as he prepared dinner. The smell of garlic and fresh herbs filled the air, a simple, yet perfect end to a day filled with love, reflection, and the promise of the future.

In the distance, the sound of the old clock tower's chimes rang out, marking the passing of time. But for Camille and Jules, time no longer had power over them. They had made their own future—a future that was just beginning

Chapter 13

ECHOES OF THE PAST

The soft hum of the town of Colmar filled the air as Camille and Jules wandered through the narrow streets one crisp autumn evening. The leaves crunched underfoot as they strolled, hand in hand, under a sky painted with shades of orange and pink. The town had settled into a quiet, familiar rhythm, and yet, there was a feeling in the air—something that tugged at Camille's heart, a whisper of something unfinished, as though the past still had a presence in their lives.

Jules, sensing her quiet contemplation, glanced at her, his eyes filled with concern. "What's on your mind, love?"

Camille paused, her gaze lifting to the towering figure of the clock tower looming in the distance. The sight of it always made her heart flutter, a reminder of the promise she had helped fulfil, of the

love that had transcended time. But tonight, it felt different—distant, almost like a forgotten memory from another lifetime.

"I don't know," she replied softly, her voice laced with uncertainty. "It's just... sometimes, I still feel the pull of the past. The echoes of Élise and Jules are so deeply woven into this town. I wonder if we'll ever be completely free of them."

Jules slowed his pace and came to a stop beside her, his expression thoughtful. "I understand. It's hard to forget something that has been a part of us for so long. But you've done something incredible, Camille. You've not only helped me find peace, but you've also given that peace to Élise. That's something no one else could do."

Camille sighed, her fingers brushing the edge of the pendant around her neck—an heirloom from her grandmother, a constant reminder of the love she had found with Jules. "I know, but I can't help feeling like there's still something we're missing. Something unfinished, even after all we've been through."

Jules gave her hand a reassuring squeeze, his touch grounding her. "Maybe it's not about completing the past. Maybe it's about making sure the present is enough."

She nodded slowly, the weight of his words settling into her heart. Perhaps the final piece of their story was not about erasing the past, but about embracing what they had now, what they had built together. The love they shared wasn't bound by time—it was anchored in the present, in the choices they made each day to move forward together.

Later that evening, after dinner, Camille sat at the desk, staring at the pages of her manuscript. The novel she had been working on was nearing completion, and yet, something was still missing. The love story between her characters mirrored her own in many ways, but it lacked the depth she felt in her heart. The words felt too shallow, too distant from the love she now understood. She needed to write something more—something that captured not just the romance, but the depth of her journey with Jules.

She grabbed a fresh sheet of paper and began to write. The words flowed from her, each one carrying the weight of her soul. She wrote of love that had survived lifetimes, of a journey that began with pain but ended in peace. She wrote about the power of healing, of accepting the past but choosing to live for the present.

In that moment, Camille understood. The key to freedom—both for her and for Jules—was not to escape the past, but to make peace with it. It was about acknowledging the

echoes of those who had come before them, and using that knowledge to create something even more beautiful.

The next morning, Camille stood in front of the mirror, adjusting the collar of her coat. It was the first day of November, and the air had turned crisp and cool. The town of Colmar was beginning to change, the golden hues of fall giving way to the bare branches of winter. But it was more than just the seasons that had shifted. Camille felt different. She felt complete.

Jules entered the room, a cup of coffee in hand, his usual smile lighting up his face as he caught sight of her. "You look stunning," he said, his voice full of admiration.

She smiled, but there was a new determination in her eyes. "I've been thinking," she began, turning to face him. "We've been so focused on the past—on finishing Élise and Jules's story. But I think it's time we start writing our own."

Jules raised an eyebrow, setting the coffee down on the dresser. "Our own story?"

"Yes," she replied, stepping closer to him. "It's time to stop looking back, to stop searching for something that's already gone. We have something beautiful right here, right now. And I think it's time we fully embrace it—our future."

Jules stepped forward, taking her hand in his. "I've never been more ready."

Together, they left their apartment and made their way to the town square. It was a familiar route, one they had walked countless times before. But today, it felt different. As they passed the clock tower, Camille glanced up at its towering presence. For the first time, it didn't feel like a reminder of a past love—it felt like a symbol of everything they had overcome and everything that lay ahead.

That evening, as the sky turned dark and the first stars began to twinkle, Camille sat by the window with her manuscript in hand. The words she had written were more than just a story—they were a reflection of her journey, of her love for Jules, and of the life they were building together. The past had its place, but it no longer held power over her. She had let go, and in doing so, had freed herself to live fully in the present.

Jules joined her, sitting beside her and draping an arm around her shoulders. "How's the book coming along?" he asked softly.

"It's almost done," Camille said with a smile. "And it's the most honest thing I've ever written."

"I'm proud of you," Jules whispered, pressing a gentle kiss to her temple.

As they sat there, in the quiet of the night, Camille realized that the final chapter of their story was still being written. It wasn't about completing something that had been left unfinished. It was about living fully in the now, in the love they shared, and in the future that stretched out before them.

With Jules by her side, Camille knew that the echoes of the past were only whispers now, fading with each passing day. The love they had created was strong enough to withstand anything—and it was only just beginning.

And so, with the turning of the seasons, Camille closed the book on the past and opened a new chapter, one filled with endless possibilities, as the love between her and Jules blossomed into something more beautiful than she had ever imagined.

Chapter 14
A NEW BEGINNING

The following morning, the sun rose lazily over Colmar, casting a soft golden light over the cobblestone streets. Camille stood in front of the window, gazing out at the serene town as she sipped her coffee. It was the first time in a long while that she felt at peace, truly at peace. The weight that had once hung heavy on her heart—the burden of the past, of Élise and Jules's unfinished story—was now a memory. The future stretched out before her, bright and full of promise.

She could hear Jules in the kitchen, humming softly as he prepared breakfast. The sound of his voice was comforting, a reminder of how much her life had changed since that fateful night when she had first met him at the clock tower. It had been a whirlwind of emotions, of discovery, and of healing. And now, they stood on the cusp of something new.

Camille felt a sense of excitement ripple through her as she thought about the life they were building together. It wasn't just the love they had found in each other—it was the understanding that they had given one another a second chance at happiness, a chance to create a future that was theirs alone.

That afternoon, Camille and Jules sat together at a café by the canal, the autumn leaves drifting lazily along the water's surface. The town was quiet, the hustle and bustle of daily life blending with the peaceful rhythm of the seasons.

"I've been thinking," Jules said, breaking the comfortable silence. His voice was thoughtful, as though he was carefully choosing his words. "We've both been through

so much, Camille. I feel like we've experienced a lifetime in just a few months. But I think... I think it's time we take the next step."

Camille raised an eyebrow, her curiosity piqued. "The next step?"

Jules smiled, his eyes sparkling with mischief. "Yes. We've been living in this town, in this moment, for so long. But what if we could build something new, together, somewhere else?"

Camille blinked in surprise. "You mean... move?"

He nodded. "I've been thinking about it. We've both always loved the idea of adventure, of discovering new places. And we've already started a new chapter in our lives here. But maybe it's time to create our own new world, just the two of us. Somewhere where we can build something even greater than what we've already created."

A wave of excitement surged through Camille. The idea was exhilarating, but it also made her feel vulnerable. "Where would we go?" she asked, her voice barely above a whisper.

Jules took her hand across the table, his touch grounding her. "I don't know yet. But we have the freedom to choose, to go anywhere. Maybe Paris, or a small village in the south of France. The world is wide open for us."

The thought of leaving Colmar, the place that had brought them together, was bittersweet. But Camille realized, as she looked into Jules's eyes, that home wasn't just a place. Home was wherever they were, as long as they were together.

"I'm ready," she said, her voice filled with conviction. "Let's do it. Let's build a life that's all our own."

Jules's smile widened, and he leaned across the table, pressing a gentle kiss to her forehead. "I knew you'd say that."

In the days that followed, the couple began to make plans. It wasn't easy. There were moments of doubt, moments when the weight of the decision felt overwhelming. But with each step, they grew more certain that this was the right choice. The idea of starting fresh, of carving out a new life together, was thrilling. They talked about the places they wanted to visit, the dreams they wanted to chase, and the future they would create.

Camille couldn't help but smile as she looked back on the journey they had taken. From the day she had found the letters to the night she had met Jules, everything had led to this moment. She had never imagined that her life would take such an unexpected turn, but now, with Jules by her side, she couldn't imagine it any other way.

It was the night before they were set to leave Colmar. Camille stood on the balcony of their apartment, gazing out at the town below. The lights of the clock tower flickered in the distance, a reminder of everything that had come before. She thought of Élise, of Jules, of the love that had tied them all together. And she thought of how far they had all come.

Jules joined her on the balcony, wrapping his arms around her from behind. "It's beautiful, isn't it?" he murmured, his breath warm against her ear.

"It is," Camille replied, her voice filled with emotion. "But it's time for us to go."

Jules nodded, pressing a kiss to her hair. "We've made peace with the past, Camille. Now, it's time to create our future."

As the town of Colmar settled into the quiet of the night, Camille knew that they were making the right choice. It wasn't

just about leaving—it was about moving forward, together, into a future full of possibilities.

The next morning, with their bags packed and their hearts full of hope, Camille and Jules stood at the edge of the town square. The cobblestones felt familiar beneath Camille's feet, and the sound of the town waking up around them was comforting. But the world beyond Colmar was calling to them, and they were ready to answer.

They took one last look at the clock tower, its hands frozen in time, and then turned to face the future.

With each step they took, Camille felt the weight of the past fall away. The echoes of the past had faded into the distance, and before them lay a new chapter, waiting to be written. Together, they would create a love story that was uniquely theirs—one that would carry them through the rest of their lives, wherever they went.

And so, they walked into the unknown, hand in hand, ready to face whatever the future held.

Epilogue

Years later, the town of Colmar remained a distant memory, a place they had once called home. Camille and Jules had built a life together in a small village by the sea, surrounded by the beauty of nature and the peace of their shared love. The clock tower in Colmar, frozen in time, was no longer part of their story. But their love, their journey, and the life they had created together—those would never be forgotten.

In the quiet of their new home, Camille sat at her desk, writing the final chapter of her novel. The story she had written was no longer about the past—it was about the future, about the love she and Jules had shared and would continue to share for the rest of their lives.

As she closed her laptop, Camille smiled. The story was complete. And the greatest love story of all was still being written

THE QUIET GOOD BYE

Chapter 1

A MEETING IN EXILE

Vienna, 1920. A city of fading imperial grandeur and rising modernism, caught between the remnants of the old world and the uncertain promise of the new. The streets hummed with the energy of reinvention, where the shadow of war still clung to every corner, and the promise of change danced through the air like an elusive dream. It was here that Aleksandr Petrov, a Russian émigré, found himself adrift, a man without a country, seeking solace in a city that was both foreign and familiar.

His exile had not only uprooted him from his homeland but had also severed his connection to the life he once knew. The revolution had swept everything away, and Europe had become his refuge—a transient home where fragments of his past lingered like ghosts. It was in this place, among other displaced souls, that Aleksandr first met Sofia.

Sofia was unlike anyone he had ever encountered. With a quiet elegance and a mysterious allure, she commanded attention without needing to try. Her deep blue eyes seemed to carry untold stories, stories that Aleksandr longed to understand. Yet, it was not only her beauty that captivated him; it was the way she moved through the world, her thoughts drifting in and out like a delicate melody. She was a puzzle, one that Aleksandr couldn't quite solve, though he was undeniably drawn to it.

Their first encounter occurred at a gathering in a modest café, filled with fellow émigrés, intellectuals, and artists. Sofia sat at a corner table, her presence blending effortlessly into the lively atmosphere. Her laughter rang out like a clear bell amidst the boisterous chatter, but Aleksandr couldn't help but

notice the way her gaze often wandered, as if searching for something beyond the conversation at hand.

As the evening wore on, they found themselves speaking, drawn together by a shared sense of displacement. Sofia was keenly aware of the political and social upheavals of the time, yet she spoke with a certain detachment, as if keeping her distance from the world she now inhabited. Aleksandr, in turn, was struck by her poise, her intelligence, and the subtle sadness that lingered just beneath her surface.

It was during this brief exchange, as the night drew to a close, that Sofia proposed an unexpected challenge.

"Aleksandr," she said, her voice calm but decisive, "I have a proposition for you."

He raised an eyebrow, intrigued. "A proposition?"

"Yes," she replied, her lips curving into a small, knowing smile. "I want you to write to me. But there's one condition."

Aleksandr leaned forward, curiosity piqued. "What condition?"

"You must not write to me about love," Sofia stated firmly, her eyes meeting his with an intensity that caught him off guard. "Not a word. No letters about love, nothing at all."

Aleksandr blinked in surprise, then let out a soft laugh. "You ask for the impossible. How can one write without love?"

"That is your challenge," she answered, her voice unwavering. "To write about life, about the world, but not about love. Not a single mention."

For a moment, Aleksandr was taken aback. The idea seemed both absurd and strangely alluring. How could one write about everything except the very thing that dominated the

heart and mind? And yet, there was something about Sofia's proposition that sparked a sense of adventure within him.

"Very well," he said with a smile, a hint of intrigue in his voice. "I accept."

With that simple agreement, an understanding was born between them—one that would unfold in the pages of letters, each word carefully chosen to explore the world and themselves without ever acknowledging the emotions that lay at the core of their connection. In a city where so much had been lost, Aleksandr and Sofia would begin a correspondence—a game of words, a dance of restraint, where the absence of love would, in the end, speak volumes

Chapter 2
Letters Begin – Life in Vienna

Vienna, 1920. The city's grandeur had begun to fade, its imperial charm losing its luster beneath the weight of post-war austerity. The streets, once brimming with the elegance of aristocracy, now teemed with the displaced—artists, writers, and intellectuals seeking refuge in the heart of Europe. Among them was Aleksandr Petrov, who wandered through these streets as though searching for something he could not name. His footsteps echoed against the cobblestones, a rhythmic reminder of the uncertainty that defined his life.

Despite being surrounded by people who shared his sense of exile, Aleksandr could not escape the isolation that clung to him. The city, vibrant as it was, felt like a cold, distant world. And yet, there was something about Vienna that kept him tethered, a sense of continuity that kept the ache of loss at bay, if only for a moment. It was in this city that he had met Sofia, and it was now in this city that he would begin to write to her.

The first letter came unexpectedly, as if a floodgate had opened within him. The challenge Sofia had given him, though absurd, had ignited something deep within. He sat at a small desk in his modest apartment, the dim light from a nearby lamp casting shadows on the worn paper in front of him. His pen hovered over the page as he wondered how to begin. He could not write about love—so what, then, could he write about?

He wrote of Vienna, of its cafés filled with intellectual debates, the streets alive with the sounds of exiles speaking in fractured languages, trying to piece together a life that could

never truly be whole. He wrote about the city's melancholy beauty, how the ornate architecture stood as a reminder of a past that could never be reclaimed. But even as he described the city's charm, Aleksandr couldn't shake the feeling that it was all a mask, a temporary escape from something deeper.

Sofia, he wrote, would understand this. She was as much a part of this displaced world as he was, a soul adrift in the same sea of uncertainty. And yet, he knew, she would also see the small absurdities of it all—the way people clung to the familiar while the world around them continued to change. His words flowed freely, but always skirting the edges of something he could not express.

"I find myself walking through these streets, Sofia," he wrote, "and though I do not know where they lead, I cannot help but feel they are somehow leading me toward you. There is a strange comfort in this, as if the city itself is keeping us bound together. Perhaps it is simply the nature of exile—to find connection in places where connection is not supposed to exist."

He folded the letter carefully, the weight of his words settling in the silence of the room. It was not a love letter, not in the way that Sofia had feared. But it was honest, a reflection of the life he led, the world he inhabited, and the unspoken bond that was beginning to form between them.

Days passed before Aleksandr received a response. It arrived on a dreary afternoon, the envelope bearing Sofia's elegant handwriting. He tore it open quickly, eager to know how she would reply to his observations, his reflections. Her words, when they came, were not as he had expected. She did not address his thoughts directly, but rather, she spoke of something else entirely.

"Vienna is a city of masks, Aleksandr," Sofia wrote. "Everyone here wears one—perhaps it is the only way we can

survive. But what happens when the masks fall? What do we find beneath them? Or do we simply become the masks themselves?"

Her letter was brief, but the question lingered in his mind long after he had read it. Sofia, even in her indirect way, had struck a nerve. The idea of masks and facades—the way people hide their true selves in plain sight—resonated deeply with Aleksandr. He wondered if he, too, was wearing a mask. Could he truly write about life without touching upon the emotions that swirled just beneath the surface?

But Sofia's words, though cryptic, had an unexpected effect. They stirred something within him, a deeper curiosity about the woman who had challenged him to write without love. It was clear now that she was not interested in the superficialities of human connection. She wanted something more. Perhaps, he thought, it was not love that she sought, but truth.

In his next letter, Aleksandr focused less on the city and more on the people who inhabited it. He wrote about the fellow émigrés he encountered—artists, writers, and philosophers—each of them carrying the weight of their pasts in different ways. Some wore their histories like badges of honor, while others, like him, tried to bury them beneath layers of self-imposed detachment.

"It is strange," he wrote, "how easily we become our own stories. We are shaped by them, but we also shape them, as though they are the only things that make us real."

As he penned these words, he realized that he was no longer writing simply to fill the pages. He was writing to understand something about himself, about the way exile had shaped him, and about the quiet connection that was growing between him and Sofia.

He sealed the letter, feeling the weight of his thoughts settling into the envelope, and sent it off. What would Sofia think of his musings? Would she find meaning in his words, or would she dismiss them as just another mask? He couldn't know. But for the first time since arriving in Vienna, Aleksandr felt as though he was no longer just an exile—he was a participant in something larger, something that transcended the boundaries of time and place.

Chapter 3
UNSPOKEN TRUTHS

Vienna, 1920. The winter months brought with them a harsh, biting cold that settled over the city like a thick blanket. The once bustling streets, now covered in snow, seemed to retreat into themselves, as though even the city was trying to hibernate from the harsh realities of the world. Aleksandr found himself walking through these streets more often now, the cold air a constant reminder of the emotional chill that had taken hold of his life.

His letters to Sofia had become a ritual, a way to wrestle with the solitude that defined his existence in exile. But as the weeks passed, the act of writing began to feel like a bridge—fragile, but important—stretching out between them. He no longer wrote merely to fulfill her challenge. Each letter became an attempt to understand the world he found himself in, to make sense of the uncertainty, and to explore the strange bond that had developed between him and Sofia.

The correspondence had a rhythm to it now—one that moved in fits and starts, like an old song trying to find its tempo. The letters were less about the city and more about their thoughts on life, philosophy, and the quiet, unspoken truths that seemed to hover just out of reach. Aleksandr had begun to wonder whether they were speaking to each other through the words that weren't written as much as the ones that were.

In his latest letter, Aleksandr wrote about something that had been occupying his mind for days: the idea of identity. Who were we, really, once all the superficial trappings of life

had been stripped away? Was there anything left when we had nothing but the memory of our pasts to guide us?

"I've been thinking about identity," Aleksandr wrote. "The way it shifts, sometimes imperceptibly, as if it were a shadow we can never quite catch. Here, in Vienna, we are all ghosts of something we once were. Some of us have embraced our new lives, while others cling desperately to what we've lost. But what are we, Sofia? What are we without the roles we used to play, the lives we used to lead?"

He paused, wondering if Sofia would think his musings too abstract. But then, he realized that it didn't matter. The challenge of writing without love, without sentiment, had already led him down a path of self-exploration, one he could not easily abandon.

He sealed the letter and sent it off with the usual sense of anticipation. What would Sofia say to this? Would she offer an answer, or would she simply leave him to his thoughts, as she often did?

A week passed before the response arrived. Sofia's letters were never rushed. They came when they came, always meticulously crafted, each word carefully chosen, as though she was weighing the significance of everything she wrote. Her letter arrived on a pale morning, the sunlight filtering through the gray clouds that hung low over the city. Aleksandr opened it, eager to read her thoughts.

Her reply was short but striking in its simplicity.

"Identity is a mask," she wrote. "It's a performance, a role we take on so others can see us for what we want to be. But beneath that mask, there is something much deeper, something we can't always express, something we often don't even understand ourselves. In exile, we are stripped of those masks.

And in the absence of them, we are forced to confront the things we've buried deep inside."

Aleksandr felt a stirring within him as he read her words. It was as if Sofia had understood exactly what he was trying to say, even without him fully articulating it. She had grasped the core of his thoughts, offering a perspective that was both liberating and unsettling.

For days, he mulled over her reply, unsure whether to send another letter immediately or to give it time to sink in. He could feel her presence in his thoughts, like a shadow in the corner of his mind, guiding him toward truths he hadn't been ready to face.

Several days later, Aleksandr sat by the window, staring out at the snowy streets below. It had been a while since he had ventured out into the city. He had grown accustomed to the solitude of his apartment, to the quiet that filled the space where the noise of the world once was. But as he sat there, he realized how much he longed for connection, for something beyond the written word, for something that could not be confined to letters.

And yet, even as the thought crossed his mind, he knew that Sofia was as elusive as ever. She was a woman who existed in the space between words, a presence that could never be fully captured on paper.

He picked up his pen again, his hand trembling slightly as he wrote. This time, his words were not as philosophical as before, nor were they focused on the city or the abstract concepts that had preoccupied him. Instead, he wrote about something far more personal, something that, until now, he had been unwilling to confront: the absence of love.

"I have thought about love," he wrote, "about how we avoid it, how we think we can live without it. Perhaps, in exile,

we convince ourselves that we are beyond it. But it's impossible, isn't it? The world may be cold, but love is a fire that keeps us warm, even if we refuse to acknowledge it. Perhaps that is why we are all so lonely here. Perhaps it's not the city, or the war, or the loss of our country that hurts the most. Perhaps it is the fact that we are still capable of love, but we have forgotten how to give it."

He paused, unsure of whether to send the letter. But in the end, he knew he could not keep these thoughts to himself. Sofia had opened a door within him, one that he had long tried to keep closed. It was time to step through it, even if it meant facing the vulnerability that came with it.

He sealed the letter, feeling the weight of his admission pressing against him. What would Sofia think of this? Would she dismiss it, as she had dismissed so many of his earlier reflections? Or would she see something in it, something he had not yet fully understood himself?

Chapter 4

BETWEEN THE LINES

Vienna, 1920. The early days of spring brought with them an unusual warmth, though the city was still haunted by the remnants of winter. The cobblestone streets, once slippery with ice, now glistened with the hint of sunlight, and Aleksandr felt the change as he wandered through the streets. It was not just the weather that had shifted, but something more subtle—a shift within him that he had not anticipated.

For weeks, his letters to Sofia had been his only form of communication with the world beyond his small apartment. But recently, he had begun to feel the weight of their silence, a silence that was heavy with unspoken words and unacknowledged emotions. Their correspondence had moved from abstract reflections to deeper, more personal admissions. And yet, there was something between the lines that neither of them had dared to confront—a quiet tension that neither had fully acknowledged, though both felt it.

Aleksandr sat in his apartment one evening, a letter from Sofia in front of him. Her words had arrived only days before, but already, they seemed to haunt him. In her letter, she had continued their conversation about identity, but this time, there was something more—something he could not quite place. Her writing had taken on a different tone, one that felt more intimate, yet still distant.

"I've been thinking about love, Aleksandr," she had written. "You speak of it as though it is something lost, but I wonder if it's always been there, lurking in the shadows. Perhaps we simply don't know how to see it for what it is.

Perhaps it's not about giving love, but recognizing it when it's right in front of us."

Aleksandr reread these words several times, trying to understand their meaning. Had Sofia, too, been grappling with the same thoughts? Or was she, as she often was, simply offering a reflection on something she had observed in others, a philosophical observation rather than a personal confession?

He closed the letter slowly, setting it down on the table beside him. The words lingered in his mind, stirring something deep within him. Was love truly a thing that could be found in the shadows, or was it something that required a clear, unmistakable recognition? He had been so sure that love was something that could be lost—something that could slip away like sand through fingers. But now, Sofia's words were making him question everything he had believed about it.

As the days passed, Aleksandr found himself returning to Vienna's cafés, seeking the solace of the familiar routine. The cafés were filled with people who, like him, were exiled from their homelands, displaced by the ravages of war. They spoke in hushed tones, sharing their stories of loss and survival, their words as fragmented as the lives they led. It was in these moments that Aleksandr found a kind of comfort, though it was fleeting. He was not alone in his isolation; there was something universal about the pain that clung to the people around him.

One afternoon, he sat at his usual table in a small café near the university, watching the world go by. The sun was beginning to set, casting long shadows across the streets. As he stirred his coffee absentmindedly, he thought of Sofia. Her presence, though distant, was always there, a constant companion in his thoughts.

Her letter had unsettled him, but it had also brought a certain clarity. She had been right, of course—love was not

something that could simply be given or received. It was something far more complicated, far more elusive. And perhaps, in the end, it was not about love at all. Perhaps it was about recognition, about seeing the other person not as an object of affection, but as a person who, like him, was trying to make sense of the world.

A week later, another letter arrived from Sofia. The envelope was slightly crumpled, as though it had traveled a long distance, and the handwriting on the front was more hurried than usual. Aleksandr tore it open, eager to see what Sofia had written in response to his last letter.

Her words were shorter this time, more direct.

"I think we are both trying to understand love, Aleksandr. But perhaps we are asking the wrong questions. Perhaps love is not a thing to be defined, but something to be experienced. Maybe it's not something we can control, but something we must allow to come to us when we are ready for it."

Aleksandr paused as he read these words. There it was again—something beneath the surface, something unspoken, that seemed to echo his own fears and uncertainties. Love was not something they could control, not something they could define in neat, tidy sentences. It was something that came when it came, a force beyond their comprehension.

For the first time, Aleksandr allowed himself to truly consider the possibility that love was not something he had lost, but something he was yet to understand. And perhaps, in understanding it, he would come closer to understanding himself.

He sat back in his chair, his thoughts swirling around him. Sofia had been right. It was not about giving love, or even receiving it—it was about recognizing it, about allowing it to

exist in its own form, without the need for definition or explanation.

That evening, Aleksandr found himself in a quieter part of Vienna, a place he rarely visited. He wandered the streets, his mind consumed by Sofia's words, by the questions she had posed, and by the sense that something was slowly shifting within him. The city around him felt different now—less foreign, more familiar. For the first time since arriving in Vienna, he did not feel quite so alone.

He stopped outside a small bookstore, its window display filled with volumes of poetry and philosophy. He had always been drawn to books, to the way they offered a glimpse into other lives, other worlds. But tonight, the books seemed to mock him. They offered answers that he knew he would never find. He didn't need answers anymore. He needed something more—something that only Sofia, in her own way, could provide.

As he stood there, lost in thought, the door to the bookstore opened, and a woman stepped out, her face momentarily illuminated by the streetlamp above. It was a fleeting moment, but it felt significant, as though the world had aligned in some small way, offering a sign he couldn't yet understand.

And then, just as quickly, she was gone—vanishing into the night, like a ghost in a dream.

Aleksandr stood there for a long time, contemplating the brief encounter, feeling as though something had just slipped away from him—something that could not be captured, something that was never meant to be understood.

Chapter 5

Echoes of the Heart

Vienna, 1920. Spring had begun to stretch its limbs across the city, bringing with it a kind of hesitant optimism. The days grew longer, the air warmer, and yet, Aleksandr still felt a certain chill inside, one that no amount of sunlight or fresh air could dispel. There was an emptiness that had settled within him, a quiet ache that seemed to mirror the season itself—a time of change, but still lingering in the past.

He had continued to write to Sofia, of course. Each letter, each word carefully considered, seemed to weigh him down more than the last. It was not the act of writing that troubled him—it was the silence between the lines, the things neither of them dared to speak aloud. Their correspondence had become more than a mere exchange of words; it had become a kind of slow, unspoken dance, a test of patience and restraint. They were both inching closer to something, but neither seemed ready to cross that invisible line that separated them.

Aleksandr sat by the window one afternoon, watching the crowds below as they moved like waves in the spring breeze. He had been here for almost six months now, and yet, the city still felt foreign to him. The faces that passed by were strangers, their lives unfolding in ways he could never know. He wondered if Sofia felt the same in her own city, wherever she was. Had exile made them all the same—outsiders in a world that no longer felt like home?

His latest letter to Sofia had been difficult to write. He had been wrestling with something for weeks now, a question that had been gnawing at him, but one he was not ready to face directly. But the weight of it had grown too heavy to ignore.

"I think we are afraid of love," he had written. "Perhaps we are afraid to let it in, because in the end, it will only leave us. We tell ourselves that it is better to remain untouched, to not care, to be indifferent. But deep down, I know that this is a lie. We fear it, not because we don't want it, but because we are not sure we can survive it. The way love demands everything, and then leaves nothing in return."

He had paused before sealing the letter, unsure if he had said too much, or not enough. But there it was, his truth, raw and unfiltered.

Days passed before Sofia's reply arrived. When he finally opened the letter, he was surprised to find it written in a different tone than usual—more vulnerable, yet equally guarded. Her words were deliberate, measured, as if she had spent hours choosing the right ones.

"I have been thinking about your words," she wrote. "You are right, in a way. Love is terrifying. It requires us to surrender, to give up control. But perhaps that is why we are so drawn to it. We are not meant to control everything. And yet, we try. We try to keep it at arm's length, to hold it at bay, afraid of what it might do to us. But love is not something that leaves us untouched, Aleksandr. It leaves its mark, whether we want it to or not."

Aleksandr felt the weight of her words settle in his chest. There it was again—an unspoken truth, one that neither of them was quite ready to accept but both understood all too well. Love was a force that could not be contained, could not be controlled, and yet, it demanded everything. And perhaps, that was what made it both so alluring and so terrifying.

He sat back in his chair, staring out at the city. The letter had unsettled him, but it had also given him something to hold on to—a small thread that tied him to Sofia, even in their isolation. They were both grappling with the same fears, the

same doubts. But in her words, Aleksandr sensed something else—something that he had not dared to acknowledge before.

Love was not something to be feared, he realized. It was something to be understood, to be explored. It was not the absence of pain, but the ability to endure it, to let it change you, to grow from it. It was the willingness to let someone else in, even when you knew they could break you.

A few days later, Aleksandr ventured into the city, his mind still heavy with Sofia's words. He wandered through the streets aimlessly, unsure of what he was searching for. He passed the same familiar places—the university, the cafés, the bookshops—but nothing seemed to spark his usual interest. It was as if the world had become muted, as if the colors of life had faded into a dull, lifeless gray.

His footsteps brought him to the banks of the Danube, a place he had not visited in weeks. The river, though still and quiet, seemed to hum with an energy that he could not quite explain. He stood there for a long time, watching the water move in slow, deliberate waves, each one carrying the past with it, only to be swallowed by the river's depths.

It was there, by the water's edge, that he saw her—Sofia. She was standing on the opposite bank, her figure a shadow against the light, as if she had materialized out of the very air itself. Aleksandr's heart skipped a beat, the world around him seeming to stop for a brief moment. It was impossible, of course—Sofia was hundreds of miles away. And yet, there she was, real and present in front of him, as if she had been there all along, waiting for him to see her.

For a moment, he wondered if he had imagined her. But then she turned, her gaze meeting his from across the river, and he knew, without a doubt, that she had seen him too. There was a stillness in the air between them, a silence that spoke

volumes, as if their entire conversation had led to this moment, this fleeting glimpse of each other across the distance.

But before he could move, before he could call out to her, she was gone—vanished into the crowd, just as quickly as she had appeared.

Aleksandr stood there for a long time, staring at the spot where she had been, his heart pounding in his chest. He didn't know what this moment meant, or why it had happened. But something had shifted inside him, something profound and unsettling.

He had come to the river seeking answers, but he left with more questions than ever.

Chapter 6
ACROSS THE SILENCE

Vienna, 1920. The days had stretched on, blurring together like the faded ink of a well-read letter. The city, once a canvas of opportunity and new beginnings, now felt like a quiet prison, its streets just a series of familiar routes Aleksandr had come to know too well. He continued to write to Sofia, yet the space between their words had grown colder, more distant. Each letter was an attempt to bridge the gap that neither of them could fully understand. They were both adrift, caught in a limbo of their own making, each waiting for the other to take the first step.

It had been weeks since the brief, strange encounter by the Danube—weeks since Sofia had appeared like a specter in the distance, only to vanish as quickly as she had come. The sight of her had lingered in Aleksandr's mind, refusing to let him go. Had it been a dream, a trick of the light, or something more significant? He couldn't shake the feeling that it had meant something, but what exactly, he couldn't fathom.

Aleksandr's nights had grown longer, the silence more oppressive. He had taken to wandering the streets late into the evening, unable to quiet the thoughts that kept him awake. He had come to a strange realization: it was not just the absence of Sofia that unsettled him, but the absence of himself. He had been so focused on understanding her, on grappling with the meaning of their letters, that he had forgotten to consider what he was really seeking. Was it love he longed for, or was it something else? Something more elusive, more intangible?

One evening, as the last remnants of daylight faded into dusk, Aleksandr sat in his favorite café, nursing a glass of wine

that had long since turned cold. The room around him was quiet, the usual hum of conversation muted. The waiter glanced at him with a look of polite indifference before moving on to the next table. Aleksandr's eyes wandered across the room, but his mind was far from here, lost in the labyrinth of his thoughts.

His fingers moved slowly over the pages of a book he had picked up, though he had no interest in reading. His eyes lingered on the words, but they meant nothing. He was waiting for something—waiting for a message, a sign, anything that would help him make sense of the chaos inside him.

It was then that he noticed her.

Sofia stood in the doorway, her figure framed by the soft glow of the streetlamp outside. Her gaze met his almost immediately, and for a moment, neither of them moved. It was as though the world had paused, giving them this brief, fragile moment of clarity. He couldn't understand it—how had she found him, and why now, after all this time?

She hesitated for a split second, then walked toward him. Her movements were deliberate, calm, as though this was something that had been planned, though Aleksandr knew it had not.

"Sofia," he whispered, his voice barely audible, as if speaking her name aloud would shatter the fragile reality of the moment.

She smiled faintly, a smile that was both knowing and uncertain. "Aleksandr," she replied softly, sitting across from him without waiting for an invitation. The weight of her presence in the room seemed to fill every corner, every space between them.

The silence that followed was not uncomfortable, but it was thick with unspoken words. Sofia folded her hands in front of her, her eyes fixed on him as though she were waiting for him to say something first. But Aleksandr found that he could not speak. There was too much to say, too much that had been left unsaid for so long.

Finally, Sofia broke the silence, her voice gentle yet firm. "You were right," she said. "We are afraid of love. But it's not just the pain we fear. It's the vulnerability. To love someone is to open yourself to them completely. And that, I think, is what terrifies us most."

Aleksandr looked at her, his heart beating faster. Her words echoed his own thoughts, thoughts that he had never dared to voice before. "I've been afraid, too," he admitted quietly. "I thought I could control it, keep it at a distance. But it's not something you can control, is it?"

Sofia shook her head, a sad smile playing at the corners of her lips. "No, it's not. Love is something that comes and goes, like the wind. You can't hold on to it forever. But you can choose to feel it, to let it shape you, even if it's only for a moment."

Aleksandr's chest tightened as he heard her words. They were both speaking of the same thing, but it felt like they were speaking different languages, trying to make sense of a feeling that neither of them truly understood.

They sat in silence for a while, the noise of the café around them fading into the background. Aleksandr's mind raced, but his heart was still. The presence of Sofia, her mere proximity, made the world seem clearer, as though the fog that had clouded his thoughts for so long had finally begun to lift.

"I've been trying to understand everything," he said, his voice barely more than a whisper. "But I think I've been trying

to understand you, when I should have been trying to understand myself."

Sofia looked at him, her gaze soft and knowing. "We are all just trying to make sense of ourselves, Aleksandr. It's not about understanding anyone else—it's about understanding your own heart."

The words hung in the air, heavy with the weight of their shared vulnerability. Aleksandr realized, for the first time, that he did not need to understand everything. He didn't need to have all the answers. What mattered was that he was here, sitting across from Sofia, and for the first time in a long time, he felt truly present.

As the evening wore on, they continued to talk, their conversation weaving in and out of topics, some light, some heavy, but all tinged with the quiet intimacy of two people who had long since crossed the threshold of simple acquaintance. They spoke of their fears, their hopes, their dreams, but never of love directly. They did not need to. It was already there, lingering in the space between them, an unspoken truth that neither of them was quite ready to claim.

When the café began to empty and the streetlights outside flickered on, Sofia stood up, gathering her things. Aleksandr stood as well, though he did not reach for his coat. There was something he needed to say, something that had been building inside him throughout the evening.

"I don't know what this is, Sofia," he said, his voice steady but unsure. "But I want to understand it. I want to understand you. I want to understand myself."

She smiled, a soft, knowing smile that seemed to hold all the answers. "We don't have to understand it all, Aleksandr. We just have to live it."

With that, she turned and walked toward the door, leaving Aleksandr standing in the café, watching her leave. The world seemed to have shifted, if only slightly. And for the first time, Aleksandr didn't feel quite so lost.

Chapter 7
THE QUIET BETWEEN US

Vienna, 1920. The days bled into one another with the same muted tones, as though the city itself was holding its breath, waiting for something that never came. Aleksandr continued his routines—writing, walking, reading—but everything felt increasingly hollow. The encounter with Sofia had left him unsettled, but in a way that was different from before. It wasn't the unsettling sensation of confusion or longing that he had grown accustomed to; it was something deeper, more profound, like a soft but persistent ache in his chest.

The city, always buzzing with the hum of life, now seemed to pulse with an odd, distant energy. The faces he passed in the street—familiar yet foreign—held no more meaning than the cobblestones beneath his feet. His thoughts often turned back to Sofia, to her words and the weight of her silence. There was an intimacy in her absence, a kind of presence that lingered in his mind. He found himself imagining her face in the crowd, her voice in the silence of the evenings.

He had not seen her again since that night in the café. Their letters had continued, of course, but they had become more like echoes, each one trying to reach across the distance but failing to touch the other. Sofia's words, once so full of warmth and life, had started to carry a certain coldness. She seemed distant in them, as if retreating into herself.

It was a rainy afternoon when he received the letter. He had been sitting by the window, watching the rain fall in slow, steady sheets against the glass, when the postman's knock interrupted the quiet. Aleksandr opened the door to find a thick envelope in his hands—more than just the usual brief

correspondence. The handwriting on the front was unmistakable.

***Sofia**.*

With a sense of hesitation, he tore open the envelope, his heart beating a little faster, as though he were anticipating something significant. The letter inside was longer than usual, its contents dense with meaning. He began to read, his eyes tracing the words carefully, trying to capture the essence of what she was saying.

Aleksandr,

I find myself at a crossroads, though I cannot explain why it feels like a decision has already been made. Perhaps I've known for a long time that this would come to pass, and yet I'm still unsure of what it means. I can hear the silence between us growing louder with each passing day, and it fills me with an odd sense of relief. I am no longer afraid of it. In fact, I think I have learned to accept it. The truth, I think, is that I do not need to speak with you to understand you. There is a kind of knowing in silence, don't you think? But I need time now. Time to think. Time to be. So, I write this not as a farewell, but as a pause—a necessary one for both of us.

Yours, always,
Sofia

Aleksandr sat for a long time, staring at the letter in his hands, the words swimming in front of him like a distant memory. The weight of what she had said settled on him, heavy and still. A pause. She had asked for space, for time to think, but the way she spoke of it—it was as though she were pulling away, not out of fear, but out of a kind of quiet certainty. There was no urgency in her words, no plea for him to understand. She had already made her peace with whatever was to come.

It was strange, how someone's absence could feel more definitive than their presence. In the silence between them, Aleksandr could hear his own thoughts, clearer than ever before. He had spent so much time seeking answers, seeking Sofia's affection or understanding, but perhaps the real question had always been whether he could truly understand himself, apart from her.

He folded the letter carefully and placed it in the drawer of his desk. The room felt still, as if the letter itself had absorbed all the energy in the air. He had no answer to give her, no words to offer that could unravel the quiet that had settled between them. But he did know one thing: he could not keep waiting for something that may never come. The silence, in all its weight and finality, had become their shared language.

Days passed, and Aleksandr continued with his life, though it had started to feel like something he was merely observing, not participating in. The world around him continued to turn, people continued to move in and out of his life, but he felt increasingly detached from it all. It was as though he were watching it all unfold from a distance, unable to connect in the way he once had.

But there were moments, brief flashes, when he would catch sight of Sofia—her image flickering like a shadow in his mind. She was always just out of reach, a reflection of something that might have been. He wondered if she, too, felt the same way, as though they were two people walking parallel paths, never quite able to meet.

One evening, as he wandered the streets of Vienna, lost in thought, he found himself outside the café where they had met so many weeks ago. The door was open, and the low murmur of conversation spilled out into the street. Something in him

stirred—an impulse, a desire to see her again, though he knew it was impossible.

He stood there for a moment, staring into the dimly lit room, before turning away. The streets of Vienna seemed to stretch endlessly before him, each one an avenue that led further away from the past, from Sofia, from everything that had come before.

That night, as he lay in bed, his thoughts wandered once more to her letter. A pause. It was as if Sofia had given him permission to stop searching, to stop striving for an answer that didn't exist. And in that pause, Aleksandr realized that perhaps there was nothing more to understand. Perhaps the silence between them was enough.

He closed his eyes, feeling the weight of the world lift off his chest for the first time in months. The quiet was no longer a void to be filled with words or questions. It had become a space for something else—something unspoken, but deeply felt.

And so, with a sense of finality, he let go of the need for resolution. For now, there would be no more letters, no more searching. There was only the quiet between them, and the acceptance that, sometimes, silence speaks louder than any words ever could.

Chapter 8

THE UNSPOKEN TRUTH

Vienna, 1921. The year had drifted into a quiet rhythm, its passing marked not by events, but by the gradual, unnoticeable changes in Aleksandr's own life. The city, once brimming with possibilities and urgency, had taken on a slower pace, as if it, too, was caught in the stillness that had settled around him. He no longer rushed through his days. He walked with the same calm precision as the people in the cafés, the passersby in the streets—their movements slow and deliberate, as if they had all come to accept that time would move at its own pace, regardless of their desires.

The letters between Aleksandr and Sofia had dwindled into mere formalities. The exchanges were polite, distant. There was nothing left to say. Sofia, too, seemed to have come to terms with the separation between them. And yet, every word she wrote carried the weight of a decision that neither of them had truly made—it was a decision made by the absence itself.

Aleksandr had tried to immerse himself in his writing. He continued with his novels, his short stories, his essays, as if to fill the void that Sofia had left. But something in his words felt empty, lacking the depth they once had. They were the same stories, the same sentences, the same themes. Yet, without Sofia, they felt unfinished, like a painting without color.

One evening, as he sat at his desk, the weight of his thoughts heavier than usual, there came a knock at the door. It was an unexpected sound, something that pulled him from his reverie, leaving him momentarily disoriented. He opened the door, half-expecting it to be the postman or a neighbor, but there, standing before him, was Sofia.

Her presence, so sudden, felt surreal, as though she had materialized out of the very air itself. She was different—softer, quieter, her eyes holding an unreadable depth. There was no apology in her gaze, no grand explanation for the years of silence that had passed between them. It was as though they both knew that no words were needed to explain what had transpired.

For a long moment, neither of them spoke. The silence stretched between them, not as an awkward pause, but as a mutual understanding—a quiet recognition of the time that had passed, and the changes it had wrought.

Finally, it was Sofia who broke the silence. "I couldn't stay away anymore," she said, her voice low, almost a whisper. "I thought I could, but I was wrong. I needed to see you again, Aleksandr. Even if it was just for a moment."

Her words, so simple yet so heavy, left Aleksandr breathless. It was the first time in a long while that he had heard her voice, the voice that had once been so familiar, now carrying a tone of vulnerability he had never heard before.

"You've come back," he replied, his voice hoarse, as though he hadn't spoken aloud in years. "But why now?"

Sofia stepped into the room, her presence filling the space between them. "Because I couldn't keep living in silence. I realized that silence, while comforting at first, only deepened the distance between us. I thought it would be enough, but it wasn't. And now, I don't know how to bridge that gap."

Aleksandr took a step closer, his gaze never leaving hers. There was a vulnerability in her that mirrored his own. For so long, he had convinced himself that he had understood everything about their relationship—that the silence between them was a choice, a mutual understanding. But now, Sofia's words were unraveling that certainty, piece by piece.

"You don't have to bridge any gap," Aleksandr said softly. "The silence between us is not something we need to fix. It just... is. And perhaps, that's enough."

Sofia's eyes searched his face, as though looking for something he couldn't give her—an answer, a solution, a promise. But Aleksandr had no answers, no clear path forward. All he had was the truth that had been lingering in the quiet spaces between them: that sometimes, silence is not an absence but a presence in its own right.

She took a deep breath, her shoulders relaxing. "I think I've always known that," she said. "But it took me this long to realize it. To understand that sometimes, we don't need to speak to understand each other. Maybe... maybe we never really needed to say anything at all."

Aleksandr reached out then, his hand brushing lightly against hers, a simple gesture, but one that carried more weight than any words could. For the first time in years, he felt something stir inside him—not the sharp pang of longing or the uncertainty that had plagued him, but a quiet, steady warmth. The warmth of understanding, of acceptance, of knowing that whatever had passed between them—whatever had been left unsaid—was enough.

As the evening stretched on, the two of them sat together in the quiet of the room, the words between them now few, but more meaningful than ever. There was no need for declarations, no need for grand gestures. They simply existed in that space together, the silence no longer something to fear, but something to embrace.

Aleksandr knew that whatever path they would take from this moment onward would not be defined by their words, but by the unspoken understanding they had found in the quiet between them. There was no need for more—only the presence

of each other, and the acceptance of the silence that had always been there, waiting for them to listen.

The days that followed Sofia's return were different, though Aleksandr couldn't quite explain how. The city of Vienna, which had once felt so distant, now seemed full of possibility again, though it was a quieter, more introspective possibility. Sofia had brought with her a peace that Aleksandr had not known he was seeking, and in her presence, he had found a way to live with the silence, to let it settle around them like a gentle cloak.

And in that silence, they began to understand something that neither of them had understood before: that the space between them was not an absence, but a presence—a presence that spoke volumes without ever uttering a word.

Chapter 9
The Thread That Ties Us

Vienna, 1921. The days after Sofia's return settled into a comfortable rhythm. They did not rush to rebuild what had been lost, nor did they attempt to force their connection into something it was not. Instead, they moved through their shared time with a quiet understanding, both aware that their bond, though once frail and distant, had become something more complex, woven from silence, words, and the passage of time.

They no longer sat across from each other at the table in their usual cafés. Instead, they met in places where the world seemed to slow down, away from the bustle of the streets and the expectations of society. They would walk through the parks on the outskirts of the city, letting the tall trees and the quiet paths wrap around them like a cocoon. There was no need to fill the silence with chatter. The simple act of walking side by side, the occasional glance exchanged, spoke volumes more than any words could.

Sofia seemed content in this new space between them, her demeanor more relaxed than when they first met, her once tense shoulders now at ease. Aleksandr, too, had changed—there was a new calmness in him, a sense of acceptance that had been absent before. He no longer felt the need to solve everything, to push for answers. Instead, he had learned to live with uncertainty, to accept that some things could not be forced into clarity.

It was on one of these walks, as the sun began to dip below the horizon, casting a golden light across the city, that

Sofia stopped and turned to him. Her face, usually so guarded, now held a quiet resolve, as though she had come to a decision that she had been carrying for a long time.

"There's something I've been meaning to tell you," she said, her voice soft but steady. "Something I've thought about for a while now."

Aleksandr stopped walking, turning to face her. His heart quickened, but he held his composure. He had learned not to fear her words, no matter how heavy they might seem. In the silence between them, there was an understanding that this moment, too, was a part of their shared journey.

"What is it?" he asked, his voice calm, though his mind raced.

Sofia took a deep breath, her eyes searching his as if trying to find the right way to say what had been on her mind for so long. "I've been thinking about how we were—how we used to be. And how different things are now. And I've realized that... I don't know where we go from here, Aleksandr. I don't know if there's a future for us, in the way we once thought there might be."

Aleksandr felt a pang in his chest. He had not expected her words to feel like this—so final, so uncertain. But there was no panic in him, no overwhelming urge to change her mind. Instead, he simply nodded, allowing the weight of her words to settle in him.

"I think I understand," he said quietly. "We've both changed, haven't we? What we wanted once, what we thought we needed... it's different now. And that's okay."

Sofia's eyes softened at his response. "I'm glad you understand. I didn't want to hurt you, but I couldn't keep pretending that things were the same. I thought time apart

would make it clear what I truly wanted, but it hasn't. Instead, it's shown me that sometimes, the most important thing is not to hold on to what once was, but to let go of it."

Aleksandr stood silently for a moment, his gaze fixed on the ground, before lifting it to meet her eyes. "You're right. I don't think either of us can go back to what we had before. We've both changed too much for that. But I don't think we need to go backward to find meaning in what we shared. Perhaps it's enough to just... be."

Her gaze softened, and she stepped a little closer to him, the space between them shrinking just enough that their presence felt solid and real. "You've always understood things better than I have, Aleksandr. I admire that about you. And I've always been afraid of change, of the unknown. But I think I'm ready now. Ready to move forward, even if I don't know what that looks like yet."

The air between them was thick with unsaid words, but neither of them felt the need to break the silence. They had come to an understanding, without the need for explanation or resolution. It was enough to acknowledge that they had grown apart, but that they had also grown together in ways they hadn't expected.

The next few weeks passed in a haze of contentment, though tinged with a subtle sadness. Sofia was still a part of his life, but no longer in the way she had once been. There were no promises of forever, no assurances that they would always be there for each other. But there was something deeper now—a mutual respect for the space they both occupied in each other's lives, without the need to define it.

One evening, as they sat together by the window, watching the city lights twinkle in the distance, Sofia turned to him, a faint smile on her lips. "I think we've both been

searching for something all this time. But maybe the real answer is that we don't need to search anymore."

Aleksandr looked at her, his expression unreadable for a moment, before it softened into a smile. "Perhaps that's the answer. Not to search, but to simply be."

And so, the quiet between them continued, not as a sign of what was lost, but as a testament to what they had found. Their connection had never been about grand gestures or declarations—it had always been about understanding, about finding meaning in the moments that didn't need to be explained.

As the days turned into weeks, and the weeks into months, their lives continued on separate paths, but in some small way, they always remained connected. Sofia had found her own space in the world, and Aleksandr had returned to his writing, no longer burdened by the need to define his life through her, but rather through his own journey.

They still met occasionally, in quiet moments, without the weight of expectation. There were no more questions between them, no more trying to force meaning into something that had already been understood. Their connection was no longer about what they had once wanted, but about what they had created together—something simple, yet profound, that neither of them had ever anticipated.

And as the years passed, both Sofia and Aleksandr carried with them the quiet understanding that sometimes, the most important things in life were those that were left unsaid—the bonds that were formed not through promises, but through the mere act of being.

Chapter 10
THE QUIET GOODBYE

Vienna, 1922. The air had shifted again, subtly but unmistakably. Aleksandr had become accustomed to the rhythm of his life without Sofia in the same way he had once known her presence, and now, there was a quiet sort of peace in the absence of expectation. It had been nearly a year since Sofia's return, and as the seasons had changed, so too had the landscape of their relationship. They were no longer tethered by the same force that had once pulled them together, nor did they feel the weight of loss that had defined the years of silence.

The world, in its own way, had moved on. And so had they.

Yet, it was an undeniable fact that there were still moments, fleeting and almost imperceptible, when they found themselves sharing the same space—whether in the cafés where they had once sat together for hours, or in the small, quiet moments that seemed to bring them back to the simplicity of their shared past.

But something had changed. There was no longer the sharp urgency of their earlier connection. No longer the hunger for answers, or for the unspoken things that had once loomed between them. What remained was a kind of reverence for the time they had shared, without the pressure of what should come next.

Aleksandr found himself walking through the city, his thoughts lost in the familiar rhythm of the streets, the cadence of his own footsteps. The city had always been a part of him, a constant presence against which the most intimate moments of

his life had unfolded. Now, more than ever, he felt at home in its quiet corners, in its hidden paths, in its ability to remain unchanged even as everything else had transformed.

It was on one of these walks that he received the letter. The handwriting, though familiar, had taken on a new weight. It wasn't urgent, nor was it desperate. It was simply a letter, like all the others, but this time, it felt different. It held a finality that had never been there before.

Aleksandr sat on a bench, his hands gripping the envelope with a mixture of apprehension and acceptance. He knew, even before reading the words inside, that this letter would change everything. It would be the last letter, the final words they would exchange. He had felt it coming, had sensed the quiet pull of the end that was always hovering just beyond the horizon.

He unfolded the letter slowly, his fingers trembling slightly, and read Sofia's words:

"Aleksandr,

I have thought about this for a long time, and I hope you understand. Our time together, the space we shared, the quiet that we grew into—it has been everything I never knew I needed. But now, I find myself standing at a crossroads, and I have come to realize that it is time for me to step away completely.

I am leaving Vienna, not because I want to forget you, but because I need to. There are parts of me that have remained suspended in the past, parts that I need to let go of in order to move forward. I have spent so long holding on to what we were that I forgot what I might become.

I hope you understand that this is not goodbye forever. It is simply goodbye to the version of us that has lingered

between us for so long. Perhaps, someday, we will meet again. But for now, I must say goodbye.

Yours, Sofia"

The letter slipped from Aleksandr's hands, falling to the bench beside him. His heart felt heavy, but not with sadness. Instead, there was a quiet resignation, a kind of finality that he had known would come, even if he hadn't wanted it. He knew that Sofia had found her way to the answer he had come to long ago—the answer that had been simmering between them for months: they had come to the end of their shared story.

The decision to leave wasn't a dramatic one for Sofia. It was not marked by anger or heartbreak; it was simply a quiet realization that she needed to let go. In a way, Aleksandr had already let go, even before she had put it into words. Their connection had always been frail, hanging by the thinnest thread, and now that thread had been severed.

The days that followed were filled with a strange kind of quiet. Sofia's absence was not marked by the usual pangs of grief or the unbearable ache of missing someone. Instead, Aleksandr moved through his life with a peaceful acceptance, as if the space she had occupied had simply returned to him, a space he could fill with his own thoughts once again.

He did not search for her. He did not try to understand what she had meant by her decision, nor did he question why she had chosen this path. The answers, in their own way, were clear. Sofia had come to the same place he had—a place of acceptance and understanding. She had chosen her own path, and he had chosen his.

One evening, as the sun began to set and the shadows of the city stretched long across the cobblestone streets, Aleksandr sat alone in his favorite café. The glass of wine before him was untouched, the words of a book he had been

meaning to read resting unopened in front of him. He simply sat, watching the world go by, letting the stillness of the moment settle around him.

And as he sat there, he realized that there was no need for grand conclusions, no need for sweeping declarations. His connection with Sofia had been real, but it was no longer his to hold on to. It was enough to know that they had shared something, even if it was fleeting. It was enough to know that they had both learned to live with the silence, to find meaning in the quiet spaces between them.

The city was alive around him, but in that moment, Aleksandr felt an overwhelming sense of peace. He had come full circle. And as the sun dipped below the horizon, casting the city in a golden glow, he smiled softly, not in sorrow, but in understanding.

CANVAS OF THE HEART

Chapter 1
THE QUIET VILLAGE

Nestled amidst rolling hills and lush green fields lay the tranquil village of Sundarvan. The village was a world of its own, untouched by the rush of modern life. Here, time moved slowly, and the simplicity of life made it a haven for those seeking peace. The mornings were filled with the chirping of birds and the soft rustling of leaves as the gentle breeze kissed the earth.

Ananya, a 21-year-old girl with a heart as pure as the morning dew, lived in a modest but cozy home at the edge of the village. Her days began with the rising sun, her delicate hands weaving garlands from the fresh flowers she picked from their garden. She loved the quiet rhythm of her life—feeding the cows, helping her mother, Sita, in the kitchen, and listening to her father, Harish, talk about the village's age-old traditions.

That morning, as Ananya stood by the small pond near her home, her reflection smiled back at her. She was dressed in a simple green saree, her long, dark hair braided neatly. Her wide, curious eyes mirrored the dreams she often nurtured silently—dreams of exploring the world beyond the hills, of a life filled with love and meaning.

As she walked back home with a basket of freshly picked flowers, she noticed her father reading a letter with furrowed brows. Harish looked up as she entered, his expression softening.

"Ananya," he began, folding the letter carefully, "We've received a proposal for you. Raghav, an engineer from the city, is coming to visit us. He's the son of my old friend Ramnath."

Ananya froze for a moment, her heart skipping a beat. The word "proposal" sent a ripple of apprehension through her. Though she had always known this day would come, the thought of leaving her village and family felt like a distant storm now suddenly upon her.

Sita, bustling in the kitchen, chimed in cheerfully. "It's a good match, Harish. Ramnath's family is respectable, and Raghav has a fine education."

Ananya forced a small smile, not wanting to dampen her parents' excitement. But inside, she felt a whirlwind of emotions. She had never even met this man. Would he understand her love for the simple joys of Sundarvan? Could she trust a stranger with her dreams and heart?

The rest of the day passed in a flurry of preparations. The small house was cleaned, and Harish instructed Ananya's elder brother, Vikram, to ensure everything was perfect for their guest.

As night fell, Ananya lay on her bed, staring at the wooden beams of the ceiling. The quiet of the night only amplified her thoughts. Little did she know, the arrival of a stranger in her life would not only alter her destiny but also bring an unexpected twist that her heart would find impossible to resist.

The village of Sundarvan slept under a blanket of stars, unaware of the story that was about to unfold—a story of love, misunderstandings, and the delicate threads that bind hearts together.

Chapter 2

HARISH'S DILEMMA

The next morning in Sundarvan dawned with a golden hue spreading across the fields. Harish sat on the verandah, sipping his morning tea, the letter from Ramnath still on his mind. It was rare for such an opportunity to come by—a well-educated city engineer showing interest in a girl from their modest village. For Harish, this proposal was not just about Ananya's marriage; it was about securing her future and elevating the family's standing.

Inside the house, Sita was already busy with her chores, humming a tune as she prepared breakfast. Ananya joined her quietly, her mind still occupied with thoughts of the stranger who was to visit. She hadn't dared to voice her worries, knowing her parents' happiness depended on her agreement.

"Ananya, help me make the sweet dishes," Sita said with a smile. "We must leave a good impression on Raghav when he arrives."

Ananya nodded, her hands mechanically kneading the dough for the laddoos. Her heart wasn't in it, but she couldn't bear to disappoint her parents.

Meanwhile, Harish was thinking of the upcoming visit. Though Raghav's father, Ramnath, had assured him of his son's character, Harish couldn't help but worry. Would Raghav, a man accustomed to city life, truly appreciate the simplicity of Ananya and their village? Would he see her for who she really was—kind-hearted, humble, and deeply rooted in tradition?

As he sat lost in thought, Vikram approached him. "Baba, don't worry too much," Vikram said, sensing his father's unease. "Ramnath uncle's family is respectable. If his son is anything like him, Ananya will be happy."

Harish sighed, looking at Vikram. "I know, but a father's heart always worries. I just want her to have a good life."

That afternoon, as Harish walked to the village post office to confirm the arrival date of Raghav's train, he couldn't help but feel a mix of excitement and anxiety. The villagers greeted him warmly, some even teasing him about the big event.

"Harish-ji, we hear an engineer from the city is coming to see Ananya," said the village grocer. "It's a proud moment for all of us!"

Harish smiled politely, but the pressure was mounting. He knew everyone's eyes would be on their family during this visit.

Back at home, Ananya escaped to her favorite spot—a small pond surrounded by tall trees. The water's surface reflected the sky, and the calmness helped her sort through her thoughts. She dipped her toes into the cool water, wishing she could stay in this peaceful bubble forever.

"Will he understand me?" she wondered aloud, a soft breeze carrying her words away.

The day passed in preparation and nervous anticipation. Sita worked tirelessly to clean the house and prepare the best dishes, while Harish made sure the guest room was perfect. Ananya tried to stay out of the way, her heart heavy with a mixture of dread and curiosity.

As evening approached, Harish returned with the news that Raghav would arrive in two days. The family felt a wave of nervous energy sweep through the house.

"Two days," Sita said, clapping her hands. "That's enough time to make everything perfect."

But for Ananya, the days felt like a countdown to an unknown future. She couldn't shake off the feeling that her quiet life was about to change forever.

Unbeknownst to the family, the man they were expecting wasn't who they thought he would be. Fate had already started weaving a story far more complicated and beautiful than any of them could imagine

Chapter 3

THE UNEXPECTED ARRIVAL

The sun was beginning its descent over Sundarvan, painting the sky in hues of orange and gold. The village buzzed with quiet excitement as news of the visitor spread. Harish and Vikram made their way to the small railway station to receive Raghav, leaving Sita and Ananya at home to finish the final touches of preparation.

Ananya stood by the window, her hands nervously fiddling with the corner of her dupatta. She watched as the road leading to the village stretched endlessly into the horizon, wondering who would step into their lives today.

At the station, Harish scanned the sparse crowd disembarking from the train. His eyes caught sight of a young man stepping down with a leather bag slung over his shoulder. He was dressed in a crisp white shirt and dark trousers, his demeanor calm yet confident.

"That must be him," Harish whispered to Vikram, stepping forward with a welcoming smile.

The young man noticed them approaching and greeted them warmly. "Namaste, I'm Karthik," he introduced himself.

Harish, assuming he was Raghav, extended his hand. "Namaste, beta. Welcome to Sundarvan! We've been eagerly waiting for you."

Karthik smiled politely, unaware of the misunderstanding. "Thank you. It's a beautiful place. I'm sure I'll enjoy my time here."

The trio set off toward the house, chatting about the journey and the village. Karthik's easy-going nature immediately won Harish and Vikram over. He asked thoughtful questions about the village and shared small anecdotes about his work in the city, though he kept his words humble and simple.

At home, Sita and Ananya heard the sound of the approaching cart. Sita adjusted her saree and hurried to the doorway, a mix of excitement and nerves. Ananya, however, stayed back in the shadows, her heart pounding as she heard footsteps nearing.

Karthik entered the house and folded his hands in greeting. "Namaste, aunty," he said warmly to Sita.

"Namaste, beta," Sita replied, her face lighting up with approval. She had expected someone polished, but Karthik's approachable demeanor was a pleasant surprise.

Sita quickly called Ananya. "Ananya, come greet our guest!"

Ananya stepped forward hesitantly, her gaze lowered. Karthik noticed her and gave a polite smile. Her simplicity and quiet grace struck him, though he quickly turned his attention back to Harish to avoid making her uncomfortable.

As they settled into the living room, Sita served tea and snacks. Karthik praised the delicious food, instantly earning her affection. Vikram joined them, breaking the ice with stories about village life, and Karthik listened intently, occasionally laughing at the humorous bits.

Ananya, meanwhile, stayed in the kitchen, observing the conversation from a distance. She found herself unexpectedly curious about this visitor. His kind smile and genuine interest in the family left an impression on her.

As the evening progressed, Harish felt a growing sense of pride. "This boy will fit perfectly into our family," he thought, completely convinced Karthik was Raghav.

After dinner, Karthik excused himself to rest, and Harish showed him to the guest room. The family gathered in the living room, sharing their first impressions.

"He's respectful and well-spoken," Sita said. "I think he'll make a wonderful husband for Ananya."

Ananya, overhearing this from the kitchen, felt her cheeks flush. She didn't know what to make of her feelings. There was something about Karthik that intrigued her, but she barely knew him.

In the guest room, Karthik lay on the simple cot, staring at the wooden ceiling. He hadn't anticipated such warmth and hospitality from the family. "This place feels so different," he thought. "Peaceful. Genuine."

Little did he know, the misunderstanding about his identity was about to create ripples that would change all their lives forever.

Chapter 4

A Day in Sundarvan

The next morning, Sundarvan awoke with its usual charm. The sun rose lazily over the hills, casting a soft golden light on the fields. Karthik stepped out of the guest room, greeted by the gentle aroma of fresh flowers and the distant hum of village life.

"Good morning, beta!" Harish greeted warmly, already seated on the verandah with his morning tea.

"Good morning, uncle," Karthik replied with a polite smile. "I must say, waking up here feels so refreshing. It's nothing like the city."

Harish chuckled. "That's the beauty of Sundarvan. Simplicity and peace are all we have to offer."

Sita soon joined them, bringing breakfast—hot puris and a spicy potato curry. "You must eat well, beta. You've come all the way from the city," she said, her maternal instincts in full swing.

Karthik thanked her and dug in, genuinely appreciating the homemade food. As he ate, his eyes wandered to the backyard, where Ananya was busy watering the plants. Her quiet presence seemed to complement the calmness of the village.

After breakfast, Harish suggested a walk around the village to show Karthik the place. Vikram joined them, acting as the guide. The trio strolled through narrow lanes lined with mud houses, each one adorned with colorful rangolis.

Villagers greeted them warmly, their curiosity evident in their friendly smiles.

"This is the temple," Vikram said, pointing to a centuries-old structure standing tall amidst the greenery. "It's the heart of our village."

Karthik paused to admire the temple, its intricately carved pillars telling stories of a bygone era. He felt a sense of serenity wash over him as he walked inside to offer a quick prayer.

As they continued, they passed the village school, where children were playing and reciting lessons aloud. Karthik's face lit up. "Do you help with the school, uncle?" he asked Harish.

Harish nodded. "We try to do what we can. Education is the key to a brighter future for these children."

Karthik was impressed. He respected Harish's dedication to the community and felt a growing admiration for the simplicity and values of this family.

Back at home, Ananya was busy arranging flowers for the temple. Sita noticed her daughter sneaking glances at the path leading to the house.

"Why don't you go and take tea to them when they return?" Sita teased, her voice light with affection.

"Maa!" Ananya exclaimed, her cheeks turning pink. But deep down, she couldn't deny her curiosity about Karthik.

When the men returned, Ananya brought them tea, her hands trembling slightly as she set the tray down. Karthik thanked her with a kind smile, his gaze lingering for a moment. Ananya quickly retreated to the kitchen, her heart pounding.

The rest of the day passed in casual conversations and quiet moments. Karthik found himself drawn to the simplicity of the family's life—the way they laughed, cared for one another, and valued the small joys of life.

Later in the evening, Karthik decided to explore the nearby pond he had noticed earlier. The stillness of the water, surrounded by trees, felt like a hidden oasis. To his surprise, he saw Ananya there, sitting on a rock, her toes dipping into the water.

He hesitated for a moment but then approached her slowly. "It's a beautiful spot," he said softly.

Ananya turned, startled at first, but then relaxed. "It's my favorite place," she admitted. "Whenever I feel overwhelmed, I come here."

Karthik nodded, sensing her reserved nature. They sat in silence for a while, the tranquility of the pond enveloping them. It was the kind of silence that spoke volumes—one where no words were needed to understand each other.

As the sky turned a deep orange, Karthik finally spoke. "Your family is wonderful, Ananya. I can see how much they love you."

Ananya smiled faintly. "They mean everything to me. But…" She stopped herself, unsure if she should share her feelings with a stranger.

"But?" Karthik prompted gently.

"Nothing," she said quickly, standing up. "We should head back. It's getting late."

Karthik didn't press further. He sensed there was more to Ananya than her quiet demeanor, and for the first time in

years, he felt a desire to understand someone beyond their words.

As they walked back together, a subtle connection began to form—a connection neither of them fully understood yet.

Chapter 5
A Shared Smile

The morning in Sundarvan began with a cool breeze and the chirping of birds. Karthik, feeling more at ease in the village, decided to lend a hand in the family's daily chores. He joined Harish and Vikram in the fields, where they were tending to their small wheat crop.

"You don't have to work, beta," Harish said with a laugh as he saw Karthik rolling up his sleeves.

"It's no trouble, uncle," Karthik replied, smiling. "I want to experience life here. Besides, it feels good to work with my hands for a change."

Vikram handed him a sickle, impressed by Karthik's willingness. Together, they worked under the sun, and though Karthik's city hands weren't accustomed to the labor, he didn't complain. His determination didn't go unnoticed by Harish, who began to feel an even deeper sense of trust in him.

Meanwhile, back at home, Sita asked Ananya to prepare lunch for the men. As Ananya chopped vegetables and kneaded dough, she couldn't help but think about her conversation with Karthik by the pond the evening before. His kind words and gentle demeanor lingered in her mind, stirring emotions she couldn't quite name.

When the men returned from the fields, they were greeted by the aroma of freshly cooked food. The family gathered on the floor to eat together, as was their tradition. Karthik praised the simple but delicious meal, which brought a small, shy smile to Ananya's face.

"Ananya makes the best rotis in the village," Vikram teased, making her blush even more.

"Then I'm lucky to be here," Karthik said sincerely, glancing briefly at her.

The family laughed and chatted, but there was an unspoken warmth in the room, a sense of comfort that Karthik hadn't experienced in years.

Later that afternoon, Harish suggested they visit the village bazaar to show Karthik more of Sundarvan's charm. Ananya was hesitant to join but relented when Sita insisted. The group set off, walking along the dusty paths lined with tall trees.

The bazaar was alive with color and energy—vendors selling everything from fresh fruits to handmade jewelry, children running around with wooden toys, and villagers exchanging cheerful greetings.

As the family moved through the crowd, Karthik noticed Ananya pausing at a stall displaying delicate glass bangles. She admired them quietly, her fingers brushing against a set of blue ones.

"Do you like those?" Karthik asked, stepping closer.

Ananya turned, startled, and shook her head quickly. "No, I was just looking."

But Karthik could see the truth in her eyes. Without a word, he bought the bangles and handed them to her.

"These suit you," he said simply, his voice soft.

Ananya hesitated, her cheeks turning pink, but she accepted them with a quiet "Thank you." She carefully placed them in her dupatta, her heart fluttering in a way it never had before.

The rest of the evening passed in lighthearted conversations and laughter. The family bought sweets for the house and exchanged pleasantries with other villagers. Karthik felt more connected to Sundarvan with every passing moment, its simplicity filling a void he hadn't realized existed in his life.

As they returned home under the starlit sky, Karthik walked a few paces behind the group, lost in thought. He hadn't expected to feel so at home here, nor had he anticipated the quiet pull he felt toward Ananya.

For her part, Ananya clutched the bangles tightly, sneaking glances at Karthik as they walked. She didn't know what the future held, but in that moment, she allowed herself to feel a sliver of hope.

Unbeknownst to them, fate was slowly weaving their stories together, but the shadow of the misunderstanding still loomed, waiting to unravel everything.

Chapter 6
THE SEEDS OF AFFECTION

The next day dawned with a light drizzle, the scent of wet earth wafting through the air. Sundarvan seemed even more enchanting under the overcast sky. Karthik found himself sitting on the verandah, watching the raindrops fall rhythmically onto the ground.

"Lost in thought so early in the morning?" Vikram teased, stepping outside with two steaming cups of tea. He handed one to Karthik and sat beside him.

"Just enjoying the peace," Karthik replied with a smile. "This place feels like it belongs to another world—one far away from the chaos of the city."

Vikram laughed. "That's why we love it. Here, life is simple, and happiness isn't tied to big things."

Karthik nodded, but his thoughts drifted to Ananya. Her quiet grace, her shy smiles—there was something about her that made Sundarvan feel even more special.

Inside the house, Sita and Ananya were busy preparing breakfast. Sita noticed her daughter humming softly as she worked, a rare occurrence. She couldn't help but smile.

"You seem happy today, Ananya," Sita remarked casually.

Ananya froze for a moment, then quickly said, "It's nothing, Maa. The weather is nice."

Sita chuckled but didn't press further. She had her suspicions, but she chose to let things unfold naturally.

After breakfast, Harish suggested that Karthik and Ananya visit the temple to offer prayers. "You've been here for a few days now, beta. It's tradition to seek blessings for your stay," Harish said.

Karthik agreed, and Ananya, though initially hesitant, accompanied him. The two walked silently along the path, the drizzle now reduced to a gentle mist.

When they reached the temple, the priest greeted them warmly. The ancient structure stood tall, its stone walls adorned with carvings of deities. Inside, the air was filled with the fragrance of incense and the soft hum of chants.

Karthik and Ananya offered their prayers, standing side by side before the deity. For a moment, Karthik glanced at Ananya. Her eyes were closed in quiet reverence, and a serene smile graced her lips. He felt an inexplicable sense of peace just being near her.

As they stepped out of the temple, Karthik noticed a group of village children playing under a large banyan tree nearby. Their laughter was infectious, and he couldn't resist joining them.

"Let's see if you can catch me!" Karthik called out, running into the field with the children chasing after him.

Ananya watched from the sidelines, her lips curving into a rare smile. Seeing Karthik play so freely with the children made her heart feel lighter. For the first time in a long while, she allowed herself to laugh openly.

When Karthik noticed her laughing, he paused and walked over, slightly out of breath. "Why don't you join us?" he asked, his eyes twinkling with mischief.

"I'm fine here," Ananya replied, shaking her head, though her smile lingered.

"You're missing out," Karthik teased, but he didn't push further. Instead, he turned back to the children, letting Ananya enjoy the moment from a distance.

As they walked back to the house later, Karthik said, "You should smile more often, Ananya. It suits you."

Ananya looked at him, startled by his words. She didn't respond, but her heart raced, and her cheeks warmed.

When they reached home, Sita and Harish noticed the subtle change in Ananya's demeanor. She seemed more at ease, her usual shyness replaced by a quiet glow.

That evening, as the family sat together, Karthik entertained them with stories about his life in the city. Though he kept his own struggles to himself, he shared enough to make everyone laugh and feel connected.

Ananya, sitting quietly in the corner, listened intently. She found herself hanging on to his every word, her admiration for him growing with each passing moment.

Unbeknownst to her, Karthik was beginning to feel the same. But the misunderstanding about his identity still loomed, and with it, the potential for heartbreak

Chapter 7

THE FESTIVAL OF LIGHTS

The following morning, Sundarvan buzzed with excitement. The villagers were preparing for the annual festival dedicated to the village deity, an event celebrated with great enthusiasm. The streets were lined with vibrant decorations, and the scent of freshly prepared sweets filled the air.

Harish's family was equally busy. Sita oversaw the kitchen, directing the helpers and preparing traditional dishes. Vikram took charge of organizing the evening's cultural program, while Ananya busied herself arranging flower garlands for the temple.

Karthik offered to help wherever he could, much to the family's amusement.

"You're a guest, beta," Sita said with a laugh.

"But I feel like family now," Karthik replied sincerely, which e...

Chapter 8
WHISPERS OF THE HEART

The morning after the festival, Sundarvan woke up to a serene calm. The festivities had left everyone tired but content. At Harish's house, the family sat down to enjoy a leisurely breakfast. Sita and Harish exchanged anecdotes from the night before, while Vikram teased Ananya about her dance performance.

"You stole the show, Ananya," Vikram said with a grin.

Ananya blushed and shook her head. "It was just a group performance," she mumbled.

"Well, Karthik seemed impressed," Vikram added with a mischievous glance at Karthik.

Caught off guard, Karthik coughed into his tea, earning laughter from the family. Ananya avoided his gaze, her cheeks tinged with a soft pink.

After breakfast, Harish asked Karthik if he would like to visit the nearby river. "It's a peaceful spot and one of Ananya's favorite places. You should see it before you leave."

Karthik's heart sank slightly at the reminder of his impending departure, but he nodded. "I'd love to go."

Ananya was tasked with accompanying Karthik, much to her reluctance. As they walked along the winding path to the river, the silence between them was comfortable yet charged.

The river, surrounded by lush greenery, flowed gently under the warm sun. Ananya sat on a large rock near the bank,

her dupatta fluttering in the breeze. Karthik stood beside her, taking in the tranquil beauty of the scene.

"This place is incredible," Karthik said after a while. "I can see why you like it."

Ananya nodded, her eyes fixed on the water. "It's where I come to think. Whenever I'm confused or worried, the river helps me find clarity."

Karthik turned to her, intrigued. "And are you confused now?"

Ananya hesitated, her fingers fidgeting with the edge of her dupatta. "Sometimes," she admitted.

"About what?" Karthik pressed gently.

Ananya glanced at him, her eyes searching his face. "Life," she said simply.

Karthik smiled, though he sensed there was more she wasn't saying. "I think everyone feels that way at some point. But being here, in Sundarvan, has made me realize that life doesn't have to be so complicated. It's about finding happiness in the little things."

Ananya looked away, his words stirring something within her. For a long moment, neither spoke, the sound of the river filling the silence between them.

Finally, Karthik said, "I don't want to pry, but... you seem like you carry a lot in your heart. You can share it, you know. Sometimes it helps to talk."

Ananya's grip on her dupatta tightened. "I'm not used to sharing," she said softly.

Karthik crouched beside her, his voice gentle. "Then maybe it's time you tried. I promise I'll listen."

Ananya met his gaze, and for a fleeting moment, she felt the urge to open up. But the words stayed stuck in her throat, her fears holding her back. Instead, she shook her head and stood up.

"We should head back," she said, her voice barely above a whisper.

Karthik watched her retreating figure, a pang of disappointment in his chest. But he didn't push further. He knew that trust wasn't built in a day, and he was willing to wait.

As they walked back, Karthik's thoughts were conflicted. He was growing increasingly drawn to Ananya, but the weight of the misunderstanding—the real reason for his visit—loomed over him like a storm cloud.

Unbeknownst to him, Ananya's heart was equally restless. For the first time in her life, she felt a connection that scared and excited her in equal measure. But the walls she had built around herself were hard to break.

Back at home, Sita noticed the subtle tension between the two but said nothing. She trusted that time would reveal what words couldn't.

As the day ended, Karthik sat on the verandah, gazing at the starry sky. He wondered what lay ahead for him in Sundarvan and whether he had the courage to follow his heart, even if it meant facing the consequences of the truth.

Chapter 9
THE STORM WITHIN

The peaceful days in Sundarvan seemed to stretch endlessly, and yet, Karthik couldn't shake the feeling that something was about to change. Ananya's presence, though quiet and reserved, filled his thoughts more often than he'd like to admit. Every glance, every smile from her lingered in his mind, but he knew the inevitable truth he carried with him—the letter he had yet to reveal.

It had been a few days since the festival, and the atmosphere in the house was still charged with the excitement of the celebrations. The family was busy preparing for another traditional event—one that would bring the entire village together in celebration of harvest.

On the morning of the event, Ananya and Karthik found themselves in the kitchen, helping Sita prepare the food. The kitchen was filled with the smell of freshly baked bread and spicy curries. Ananya worked with practiced ease, while Karthik tried to lend a hand, though he wasn't very skilled in cooking.

Sita laughed when he nearly spilled the pot of lentils. "Careful, beta! I think you need more practice before you can help with this."

Karthik grinned sheepishly. "I'll leave the cooking to you, Sita. I think I'm better off with other chores."

Ananya looked up briefly, her lips curving into a small smile. But she quickly looked down, her cheeks flushing slightly.

As the preparations continued, Karthik felt a strange tension in the air between them. It wasn't just the usual awkwardness that had marked their interactions earlier—it was something deeper, something unspoken that hovered between them. He wanted to bridge the gap, to tell her everything, but his own heart held him back.

Later that afternoon, after the meal was served, Harish announced that there would be a gathering at the village square for dancing and music. It was a tradition to celebrate the harvest with music, where everyone, young and old, joined in.

Karthik didn't think much of it at first, but when Ananya appeared in her dance attire, his breath caught. The simple, elegant dress she wore highlighted her grace and poise. She looked completely different—confident, vibrant, and full of life.

As she began to participate in the group dance with the other women, Karthik stood from a distance, watching her every move. He admired her from afar, but there was an unsettling feeling inside him. He couldn't deny the emotions that were slowly surfacing—the pull he felt toward her, stronger than before.

Ananya, lost in the rhythm of the music, was unaware of his gaze. The laughter and music surrounded her, and for the first time in a long time, she felt free. There was something magical about the way the village celebrated life—something she hadn't felt before.

But as the music played on, Ananya caught a glimpse of Karthik's gaze. Her heart skipped a beat, and a flutter of nervousness crept up her spine. She quickly looked away, trying to focus on the dance, but she couldn't shake the feeling that something had shifted between them.

The evening passed with lively performances, songs, and laughter, but Karthik couldn't fully immerse himself in the celebrations. His mind kept drifting back to Ananya and the silent distance between them. There was an ache in his chest, a desire to confess everything, yet a fear of the consequences.

That night, after the festivities had ended and the house settled into quietude, Karthik sat alone on the verandah, staring out into the dark sky. The moonlight bathed the house in a soft glow, but his thoughts were anything but calm.

He couldn't deny that his feelings for Ananya had grown deeper than he could have ever anticipated. She was different from anyone he had ever met—her quiet strength, her ability to find beauty in the simple things. And yet, the truth he carried felt like a storm brewing inside him, threatening to destroy everything if he didn't confront it soon.

As the night deepened, Karthik stood up and walked toward the garden, the cool breeze brushing against his face. He knew what he had to do, but he couldn't bring himself to take the first step.

He needed to tell Ananya the truth.

But how could he reveal the deception? How could he confess to her that he had come to Sundarvan under false pretenses, that his true purpose was to help his uncle's business and that he wasn't the man she thought he was?

The storm within him raged on, and he knew he couldn't keep running from it.

Chapter 10
THE CONFESSION

The days following the harvest celebration passed in a blur. The village had returned to its usual routine, but the unspoken tension between Karthik and Ananya lingered like a shadow. It seemed that the more Karthik tried to bury his feelings, the more they surfaced. Every small interaction with Ananya—every shared glance, every gentle smile—only reminded him of the truth he had yet to tell her.

One afternoon, Karthik found himself wandering through the village, lost in thought. The village was quieter than usual, with most people engaged in their own work. The golden light of the setting sun bathed the earth in a warm glow, but Karthik couldn't shake the weight pressing on his chest.

He knew it was time. The longer he delayed, the harder it would become.

His feet carried him toward the same spot by the river, the place where he and Ananya had spent a quiet afternoon together. It felt fitting—this was where their connection had first started to bloom, where he had glimpsed a side of Ananya he hadn't expected.

He waited for her, hoping that she would come by, but also knowing he could no longer avoid the inevitable.

As if on cue, Ananya appeared, walking slowly along the riverbank, her steps light and measured. She didn't notice Karthik at first, her eyes focused on the water ahead. But when she did, she froze, her heart racing at the sight of him.

"Karthik," she greeted softly, trying to sound casual, though her voice betrayed the unease she felt.

"Ananya," Karthik said, his tone steady but filled with uncertainty. He took a step toward her. "Can we talk?"

She hesitated for a moment, then nodded. "Of course."

They sat together on the same rock where they had sat before, the gentle sound of the river flowing beside them. Ananya turned her gaze to the water, not quite meeting his eyes. The silence between them stretched, thick with unspoken words.

Finally, Karthik spoke, his voice barely a whisper. "I need to tell you something, Ananya. Something that's been weighing on my heart for a long time."

Ananya looked at him, her brow furrowed in confusion. "What is it, Karthik?"

He took a deep breath, gathering the courage to speak the truth. "When I first came to Sundarvan, I didn't come here for the reasons you think."

Ananya's heart skipped a beat. "What do you mean?"

Karthik looked down, his hands fidgeting in his lap. "I wasn't sent by Harish's company. I didn't come here because of the village or the beauty of this place. I came here because my uncle asked me to investigate something—something to do with a business deal he wanted to secure."

Ananya's eyes widened, her breath catching in her throat. "So... you lied to us?"

Karthik nodded, guilt flooding his chest. "Yes. And I've been trying to find a way to tell you ever since. I never intended to deceive anyone, especially not you."

Ananya's heart raced as the truth sank in. She felt a cold chill run through her, her mind struggling to process his words. She stood up suddenly, her emotions a whirlwind inside her. "You should have told us sooner. You should have told me."

"I know," Karthik said, standing as well. "And I'm sorry. I never meant for things to get complicated. But somewhere along the way, I..." His voice faltered, and he reached out, his hand brushing hers gently. "I didn't expect to care this much. I didn't expect to..."

Ananya stepped back, pulling her hand away. "You didn't expect to what, Karthik? To feel something for me?" Her voice trembled, a mixture of hurt and confusion in her eyes.

Karthik's chest tightened. "I didn't plan for any of this, Ananya. I didn't plan to fall for you."

Ananya's breath caught, her eyes searching his face, trying to find any hint of sincerity. She shook her head, tears welling up in her eyes. "How am I supposed to trust you now? How can I believe anything you say when you've kept this from me?"

Karthik stepped forward, his heart aching as he reached out to her once more. "I understand how you feel. I know I've lost your trust, and I'm sorry. I never wanted to hurt you. I just..." He paused, swallowing the lump in his throat. "I just wanted to be with you, Ananya. But now, I realize I should have told you the truth from the beginning."

Ananya turned away, her eyes welling up with tears. "I don't know what to believe anymore." Her voice cracked as she spoke. "I've always been honest with you, Karthik. And now... now I feel like I've been living in a lie."

Karthik's heart shattered as he watched her retreating form. "Ananya, please," he called out softly, but she didn't turn around.

She walked away, leaving him standing there, alone by the river, with nothing but the weight of his confession and the sting of her rejection.

Chapter 11
THE SILENT STORM

The days after Karthik's confession passed in a heavy silence. The once lively atmosphere in Sundarvan had shifted; the village, still basking in the warmth of the harvest season, now seemed distant to Karthik. He found himself lost in thought, replaying that painful moment by the river over and over again. The image of Ananya's tear-filled eyes haunted him, making it impossible for him to focus on anything else.

Karthik had hoped that with time, Ananya would understand, that perhaps she would find it in her heart to forgive him. But each time he saw her in the village, her gaze remained cold, distant—avoiding him, as though he no longer existed in her world.

The family, especially Sita, had sensed the change in the air. Sita often looked at Karthik with a quiet concern, her eyes filled with unspoken questions. But she said nothing, giving him the space he needed. It was Harish, however, who couldn't help but notice the tension. One evening, he pulled Karthik aside as they worked on a small repair in the barn.

"Beta," Harish said quietly, "I've noticed the way things have changed between you and Ananya. Did something happen? You can talk to me if you need to."

Karthik paused, wrench in hand, his shoulders slumping under the weight of the unspoken truth. "I told her everything, Uncle. I told her about why I really came here."

Harish's face softened with understanding. "And what did she say?"

"She was upset. I can't blame her, though. I lied to her. I kept things from her, and now... now I don't know if I can fix it." Karthik's voice wavered as he spoke, the realization of his actions settling heavily on his chest.

Harish placed a hand on his shoulder. "Beta, you've done what you could. Now, it's up to Ananya. Sometimes, all we can do is give people the space they need to process. But don't give up just yet."

Karthik nodded, but even Harish's comforting words couldn't lift the weight he felt. He had betrayed Ananya's trust, and there was no easy way to make amends.

Meanwhile, Ananya struggled with her own turmoil. Her heart ached every time she saw Karthik, but she couldn't bring herself to speak to him. The confusion she felt was suffocating. On one hand, she wanted to believe him, to give him a chance to explain. But on the other hand, the hurt ran deep. How could she forgive him when everything had been built on a lie?

She spent her days lost in her work—tending to the garden, helping Sita in the kitchen, and going about her chores as if nothing had changed. But deep down, she felt a storm raging within her.

Ananya's friends, aware of the change in her demeanor, tried to console her. "You know, Ananya," one of them said gently, "you can't keep punishing yourself for something that wasn't your fault. Karthik made a mistake, but he's been honest with you now. Maybe it's time to hear him out."

Ananya shook her head, her eyes distant. "He lied to me, Meera. He lied to everyone. How am I supposed to just let that go?"

Meera sighed. "I understand. But sometimes, people make mistakes. The important thing is whether they're truly sorry, and whether they're willing to change."

The words struck Ananya deeply. She knew Karthik hadn't come to Sundarvan with pure intentions, but his sincerity in the days that followed—his struggle, his guilt—was undeniable. Still, the wound he had inflicted on her heart remained raw.

One evening, as Ananya sat by the window, watching the sunset, her thoughts drifted to Karthik. She hadn't seen him in days. He had kept his distance, respecting her space, but his absence only made her heart ache more. She had never realized how much he had come to mean to her until this silence settled between them.

But was it too late to mend what had been broken? Could she find a way to forgive him?

As if on cue, there was a knock on the door. Ananya turned to find Karthik standing in the doorway, his expression serious but gentle. She didn't say anything at first, merely watching him, the weight of the moment settling over them both.

"Karthik," she said softly, her voice barely above a whisper.

He took a step forward, his hands clenched at his sides. "Ananya, I know I don't deserve your forgiveness. But I need you to know that I never meant to hurt you. I... I've realized how much you mean to me, and I can't go on pretending everything's okay when it's not."

Ananya felt her heart race as she looked at him. "I don't know if I can trust you again," she said, her voice trembling with emotion.

Karthik's gaze softened, his voice filled with vulnerability. "I don't expect you to forgive me right away, Ananya. I just want you to know that I'm here—willing to do whatever it takes to earn your trust back. But I can't change what's happened. All I can do is show you that I care."

Ananya stood in silence for a long moment, her mind swirling with conflicting emotions. Part of her wanted to walk away, to shut the door and never look back. But another part, the part that still cared for him despite everything, wanted to listen.

Finally, after what felt like an eternity, she spoke. "I need time, Karthik. I need time to figure out what I feel and whether I can forgive you. But right now... right now, I can't give you any answers."

Karthik nodded, his expression resigned but hopeful. "I'll wait, Ananya. I'll wait as long as you need."

With that, he turned and left, leaving Ananya standing in the doorway, her heart a storm of emotions, unsure of the future but knowing that something had shifted within her.

Chapter 12
THE SLOW HEALING

The days following Karthik's visit to Ananya were filled with silence, but there was a shift in the air. Though they hadn't spoken much since that evening, the weight of unspoken words seemed to linger between them, creating an invisible bond that neither could ignore. The village continued with its daily rhythm, but there was an underlying tension, as if everyone knew that something was about to change.

Karthik had respected Ananya's request for time, giving her the space she needed. He focused on his work, spending long hours with Harish and tending to the tasks that had been left undone. Yet, his thoughts never strayed far from her. Each day, he watched as she carried on with her chores, her presence a constant reminder of his mistake and his desire to make things right.

Ananya, too, was struggling with her feelings. She had spent countless hours thinking about Karthik, about his confession, about their connection. She couldn't deny the bond they had shared—how easy it had been to talk to him, to laugh with him. And yet, his lie had left a scar, one that hadn't healed in the short span of days. How could she trust him again after everything he had kept from her?

It wasn't just Karthik's deceit that troubled her; it was the fact that she had allowed herself to become vulnerable with him, only to be hurt. Her heart ached every time she saw him, but she knew that time was needed. Time to process, time to forgive, and perhaps, time to forget the pain.

One morning, as Ananya was tending to the flowers in her garden, she noticed Karthik walking towards her from the path leading to the river. Her heart skipped a beat, but she quickly pushed aside the flutter of emotions that had surfaced. She had told him to wait, and she had to keep her distance—at least for now.

Karthik, however, wasn't deterred. He stopped just a few feet away from her, his eyes filled with a mix of hope and regret. "Ananya, can we talk?"

Ananya's fingers stilled on the petals she was gently pruning. She looked up at him, her eyes wary but not cold. "What is it, Karthik?"

He took a deep breath, his voice steady but full of sincerity. "I know I've hurt you, and I know I don't deserve your forgiveness. But I need you to know that I'm trying, Ananya. I want to show you that I'm not the same person I was when I first came here."

Ananya didn't respond immediately. Her heart was heavy with uncertainty, but she couldn't deny the sincerity in his voice. He had changed—she could see that. The carefree attitude he had when he first arrived in Sundarvan had been replaced by something more earnest, more genuine. But was that enough?

"I need time, Karthik," she said softly, her voice almost a whisper. "I can't just forget everything, and I can't pretend that it's all okay. But... I'm willing to try."

Karthik's face softened, and for the first time in days, a small but hopeful smile touched his lips. "I'll wait, Ananya. I'll wait however long it takes."

Ananya nodded, her heart still in turmoil, but there was something in his words that reassured her. It wasn't just that

he was waiting—it was that he was willing to prove his sincerity, not just with words, but with actions.

The next few days passed slowly, each moment marked by the quiet dance of tentative steps toward healing. Karthik did everything he could to show Ananya that he was trustworthy—he worked harder on the farm, he helped her with her tasks when she least expected it, and he always respected her space. Slowly, she began to see the changes in him. His smiles were no longer the charming, carefree ones he used to offer; instead, they were filled with an earnestness that tugged at her heart.

It wasn't just his actions, though; it was the way he respected her boundaries. He didn't rush her. He didn't demand her forgiveness. He simply let her know, through every action, that he was there—ready to wait, ready to be the person she needed him to be.

One evening, as the sun began to set, Ananya found herself walking along the path by the river again, the place where everything had started. She had grown accustomed to the sight of Karthik working by the water, his focus on the tasks at hand. But this time, as she approached, she saw him sitting on a rock, staring into the distance with a contemplative expression on his face.

She hesitated for a moment, then walked toward him. "Karthik?" she called softly.

He turned toward her, his eyes meeting hers with a mixture of surprise and relief. "Ananya," he said quietly, standing up. "I didn't expect you to come here."

"I've been thinking," she said, her voice steady. "About everything. About you, about me, and about us."

Karthik's heart raced, but he stayed silent, waiting for her to continue.

"I can't promise that everything will go back to the way it was," Ananya said, her gaze steady. "But I'm willing to try. I'm willing to see if we can start over, and if you're truly the man you say you've become."

A wave of relief washed over Karthik, but he didn't take a step closer. He simply nodded, his voice filled with gratitude. "I'll do whatever it takes, Ananya. I won't let you down again."

Ananya looked at him for a long moment, her heart still unsure, but open to the possibility of healing. "We'll see," she said softly, the beginning of a smile tugging at the corners of her lips. "We'll see."

As they stood there, the golden light of the sunset casting a warm glow over them, a silent understanding passed between them. They weren't yet where they needed to be, but they had taken the first step toward mending the broken trust. It was a slow healing, but it was healing nonetheless.

Chapter 13

THE FIRST SIGNS OF CHANGE

The days grew warmer as the summer arrived in Sundarvan, bringing with it a sense of renewal. The village, bathed in the golden glow of the sun, seemed to mirror the changes that were slowly taking place in Karthik and Ananya's relationship. The air felt lighter, as though the weight that had been hanging over them was beginning to lift, bit by bit.

Karthik continued to show his dedication to the work at hand, always present when needed and often going the extra mile. His actions spoke louder than words, and while Ananya had not fully forgiven him, she couldn't deny the sincerity in his efforts. There were small moments where their old camaraderie began to resurface. They shared laughs while working in the fields, and occasionally, their conversations stretched into longer talks, devoid of the awkwardness that had once defined their encounters.

One evening, after a long day's work, Karthik and Ananya found themselves walking along the edge of the river, the sound of the water's flow providing a soothing backdrop. They had been walking in silence for a while, but this time, it wasn't uncomfortable. The air between them felt different, lighter, as though they were beginning to find their way back to each other, not in the way they had once known, but in a new, more cautious rhythm.

Ananya, feeling the stillness of the moment, broke the silence. "You've been working hard," she said, her tone warm but measured. "I can see that you're trying."

Karthik glanced at her, a soft smile playing on his lips. "I don't expect anything in return, Ananya. I just... I just want to show you that I can be trusted again."

Ananya nodded, her thoughts drifting to the past. "It's not just about trust, Karthik. It's about time. It takes time to heal wounds."

"I understand that," Karthik said quietly, his gaze fixed ahead. "And I'm willing to wait, no matter how long it takes."

Ananya stopped walking and turned to face him. "I've been thinking a lot about that, about what you said. I don't know if I can just forget what happened, but..." She hesitated, as if the words were difficult to form. "But I think I'm ready to try."

Karthik's heart skipped a beat. "Ananya, if you're willing to try... that's all I can ask for."

She met his gaze, and for the first time in weeks, there was a glimmer of something hopeful in her eyes. It wasn't complete forgiveness, not yet, but it was a step forward. It was a beginning.

As the days passed, Karthik and Ananya continued their slow journey toward rebuilding what had been broken. Karthik's efforts were evident not just in his work but in the small gestures that spoke of his growing affection for her. He would bring her flowers from the field, or leave her little notes of encouragement, each one a silent promise that he was committed to making things right.

Ananya, while still cautious, began to soften. She allowed herself to be in Karthik's company more often, to share in the quiet moments they once had, and slowly, she found herself trusting him again. She hadn't forgotten the pain, but with each passing day, the hurt seemed a little less sharp.

One afternoon, as they worked together on a patch of land by the edge of the village, Ananya found herself laughing at something Karthik had said, a genuine laugh that came from somewhere deep inside her. She hadn't realized how much she had missed their easy camaraderie, the way they had once connected effortlessly.

Karthik paused, his smile wide. "I haven't heard you laugh like that in a while."

Ananya looked at him, a bit embarrassed but feeling lighter than she had in days. "I guess I've been holding back."

He nodded, a knowing look in his eyes. "It's okay. We're both still figuring things out."

The air between them felt less heavy now, their moments of shared silence no longer filled with tension but with a sense of comfort. There was an unspoken understanding between them that, while the past couldn't be erased, they could build something new, something stronger from the pieces that remained.

But just as things seemed to be moving in the right direction, a shadow from Karthik's past surfaced, threatening to disrupt the fragile peace they had started to rebuild.

One evening, a man appeared in Sundarvan, a stranger with sharp eyes and an air of authority that immediately caught the attention of the villagers. He came to the farm where Karthik was working and asked for him by name. Karthik, who had been in the middle of a conversation with Harish, turned at the sound of his name and saw the man walking toward him.

"Are you Karthik?" the man asked, his voice cold and direct.

Karthik straightened, a flicker of unease crossing his features. "Yes, I am."

The man looked him up and down, his gaze unreadable. "I've come to speak with you. It's about something from your past."

Ananya, who had been nearby, overheard the conversation. She couldn't help but feel a pang of worry. What could this man want from Karthik? And what did he mean by the past?

Karthik's expression tightened, but he nodded. "Let's talk," he said, leading the man a little away from the others.

As they walked away, Ananya watched them with a growing sense of unease. She had only just begun to let her guard down, but now, a sense of foreboding crept into her chest. What new secrets was Karthik hiding? Was there more to his story than he had told her?

Chapter 14
SECRETS UNVEILED

The sun hung low in the sky, casting an orange glow across the village as Ananya watched Karthik walk away with the mysterious man. Her heart raced with confusion and a deep sense of foreboding. Who was this stranger, and what did he mean by "something from your past"? She couldn't help but feel a twinge of unease—just when she thought she was beginning to understand Karthik, this new shadow emerged from his past, threatening to disrupt everything.

The man, tall and stern-looking, was unlike anyone she had seen in Sundarvan before. His sharp features and purposeful stride gave off an air of authority that made Ananya feel as though something important was about to unfold. Her mind raced with questions, but she stayed where she was, rooted to the spot by an instinctual sense that she was not yet meant to know everything.

Karthik and the man walked out of earshot, disappearing behind the thick trees near the river. Ananya tried to focus on the task at hand, but her thoughts kept drifting back to them. She couldn't stop herself from wondering what Karthik had been hiding all along. Had he been hiding more than just his initial mistake with her? What could he possibly be involved in that required someone like this to come to Sundarvan?

Ananya decided she couldn't stay idle, waiting for answers she might never get. She grabbed a basket and began collecting herbs from the garden, though her movements were distracted, her mind preoccupied. Every rustle of the leaves or distant footstep had her turning, half-expecting the stranger to come back and reveal the truth she feared.

Meanwhile, Karthik led the man a little further from the village, where they stopped near an old stone wall that separated Sundarvan from the untamed forests beyond. The stranger's expression remained unreadable as he glanced at Karthik with a look that seemed both disappointed and calculating.

"I didn't expect you to be hiding away in a place like this," the man said, his voice carrying an edge of accusation. "I thought you were smarter than this, Karthik. You were never supposed to come back."

Karthik's jaw tightened at the words. He had hoped he wouldn't have to confront this part of his past again, not after everything he had worked to leave behind. But now, here it was—an unwanted reminder of the life he had once known.

"I didn't choose to come back, Arvind," Karthik said, his voice calm but firm. "I never planned to come back to this life. I left it all behind, and I have no intention of returning to it."

The man, Arvind, raised an eyebrow. "You think you can just run away and forget about it all? You can't outrun your past, Karthik. It's coming for you, whether you like it or not."

Karthik's fists clenched at his sides. He had hoped that the quiet life in Sundarvan would allow him to escape, to finally heal from the scars of his former life. But now, Arvind's presence brought a flood of memories—of a past filled with lies, deceit, and dangerous choices he had made in the pursuit of power.

"I've made my choice," Karthik said, his voice cold now. "And I'm not going back. You need to leave."

Arvind smirked, taking a step closer. "You really think it's that simple? You don't control what happens next, Karthik.

You may have walked away from your past, but your past hasn't forgotten you."

Karthik stood his ground, his mind racing. He couldn't afford to let Arvind's threats reach Ananya. He had already put her through enough, and he wasn't about to drag her into the mess of his former life. "What do you want from me?" Karthik asked, his voice steady despite the storm raging inside him.

Arvind's eyes glinted with a dangerous amusement. "I want what's mine. The people you betrayed aren't going to let this go, Karthik. You think you can just hide out here and pretend none of it ever happened? I'm here to remind you that nothing stays buried forever."

Back in the village, Ananya's curiosity got the better of her. She couldn't just sit back and let Karthik carry this burden alone, especially when his past seemed so intent on catching up with him. She felt a surge of determination rise within her. She needed to understand what was going on.

Without wasting any more time, Ananya walked toward the area near the river where Karthik and Arvind had disappeared. The path was quiet, the air thick with tension as she moved closer, her heart pounding. She had to know what the stranger's visit was about.

As she neared the trees, she caught sight of the two men, their voices low but heated. She hesitated, unsure whether to approach or stay hidden, but her instincts urged her to stay. She needed to hear more.

"I can't go back to that life," Karthik said in a voice laced with frustration. "I won't."

Arvind's tone was sharp, filled with contempt. "You don't have a choice. You may think you can escape, but I'm here to make sure you don't forget where you came from."

Karthik turned away, his voice barely above a whisper. "I've done the right thing. I've changed. You can't control me anymore."

Ananya's heart clenched at the sound of Karthik's voice—tired, almost broken. She felt a deep pang of sympathy for him, but she knew she had to understand everything before she could make sense of what was happening. She needed answers.

She stepped forward, calling out to them, her voice strong despite the uncertainty churning inside her. "Karthik?"

Both men turned in surprise, their expressions shifting quickly from one of confrontation to caution. Arvind's eyes narrowed as he assessed Ananya, while Karthik's face softened, though his eyes betrayed the conflict within.

"Ananya," Karthik said, his voice low, but there was an edge of concern in it now. "You shouldn't be here."

Ananya's eyes locked onto Karthik's, her voice unwavering. "I heard enough, Karthik. What's going on? Who is this man, and why is he threatening you?"

Arvind took a step forward, his gaze flicking between Karthik and Ananya. "I'm here to remind Karthik of his past," he said, his tone cold. "You may think he's some kind of hero now, but he's nothing but a coward trying to outrun what he's done."

Ananya's breath caught in her throat, but she turned her gaze back to Karthik, her eyes filled with questions. "What is he talking about, Karthik?"

Karthik's shoulders slumped, and for the first time in front of Ananya, he seemed vulnerable—exposed. "It's a long story, Ananya," he said, his voice strained. "A story I didn't want to bring to you. But it's all catching up with me now."

Ananya's heart was heavy with a mix of emotions. She didn't know what to think or feel, but one thing was clear—there was more to Karthik's past than she could have ever imagined. The secrets were unraveling, and she was at the heart of it.

Chapter 15
The Truth Unfolds

The air hung thick with tension as Ananya stood facing Karthik and Arvind, the weight of their unspoken words pressing down on her like an invisible force. Her heart beat erratically in her chest, her thoughts racing, trying to piece together the fragments of what she had overheard. She felt as if the world around her had tilted, and everything she thought she knew about Karthik was beginning to unravel.

Karthik looked at Ananya, his eyes pleading, but he said nothing. He knew that the time had come—the time when he could no longer hide from the truth. He had tried so hard to protect Ananya from his past, to shield her from the darkness that still lingered in his life. But now, with Arvind standing there, the façade he had so carefully built was crumbling.

Ananya's voice broke the silence. "Karthik, what is he talking about? What did you do? What is all this about your past?"

Karthik hesitated, his mind racing. The words he had kept hidden for so long felt like a heavy burden on his chest. He had hoped that by coming to Sundarvan, he could leave it all behind, but Arvind's presence was a harsh reminder that the past could never truly be outrun.

Arvind, sensing the tension, stepped forward, his voice cold and deliberate. "He's a man who ran from his own mistakes. A man who betrayed the people who trusted him, and now he's hiding here, pretending to be someone he's not."

Karthik's eyes flicked to Arvind, his expression hardening. "That's enough, Arvind. I told you—I'm not going back to that life. I've changed."

Arvind scoffed, crossing his arms over his chest. "You can't change what you did, Karthik. No matter how hard you try, the past will always find a way to catch up with you. You think you can run away from it by hiding in a quiet village, but I'm here to make sure you pay for what you did."

Ananya's mind was spinning. "What are you talking about? What did he do, Karthik? Tell me the truth."

Karthik closed his eyes briefly, a wave of guilt washing over him. When he spoke, his voice was low, the words heavy with regret. "I wasn't always like this, Ananya. Before I came to Sundarvan, I was involved in things... things I'm not proud of. I made mistakes—huge mistakes. I hurt people, betrayed their trust, and got involved with dangerous people."

Ananya's breath caught in her throat, her heart aching at the rawness in Karthik's words. She had always known that there was more to him than met the eye, but she never imagined it was anything like this. "Karthik... what did you do?" she whispered, her voice trembling.

Karthik turned away, unable to meet her gaze. "I was part of a group that—" He paused, his voice cracking. "We did things for money, things that hurt others. I was blinded by ambition, by the need for power. I got in over my head, and by the time I realized what I was doing, it was too late."

Arvind's eyes flashed with something between contempt and amusement. "Too late? You didn't care back then, Karthik. You were just as willing to destroy lives as the rest of us. And now, you want to act like you're some kind of hero?"

Karthik's fists clenched at his sides, his anger flaring. "I'm not proud of what I did, Arvind. I left all of that behind. I've been trying to make amends, trying to live a better life. But I can't erase the past."

Ananya felt a wave of confusion and pain wash over her. She wanted to believe Karthik, to trust that he had changed, but the weight of his words hung heavily in the air. She had always seen him as the man who was trying to rebuild his life, but now, it seemed there was a side to him that she didn't know—a side that could not be so easily forgiven.

"You hurt people, Karthik," Ananya said softly, her voice trembling with emotion. "How do I know that you're not still hiding something? How do I know I can trust you?"

Karthik's heart twisted in his chest at her words. He understood her fear, her need for answers. He had betrayed her trust once before, and now, it seemed, the past was threatening to do so again.

"I know I can't erase the past, Ananya," Karthik said, his voice pained. "But I'm not that person anymore. I'm not. I left all of that behind because I wanted a chance to do better. I wanted a chance with you. I wanted to build something real, something honest."

Ananya stood there, torn between the man she had come to care for and the revelations that threatened to tear them apart. Her heart told her to believe in him, to trust that he had changed. But her mind, filled with doubt and questions, couldn't shake the fear that the past was too dark to be left behind.

Arvind stepped forward once more, his voice laced with mockery. "You really think she'll forgive you, Karthik? You think you can just sweep your sins under the rug and expect

everything to be fine? No one gets away with what you've done. Not even you."

Karthik's expression hardened, and he took a step toward Arvind, his voice low but firm. "I'm done with you, Arvind. If you think you can come here and ruin everything I've worked for, you're wrong. I won't let you do this."

Ananya, her emotions swirling, finally spoke, her voice a mixture of determination and vulnerability. "What do you want from him, Arvind? Why are you here?"

Arvind smirked, his eyes narrowing as he looked at both of them. "What do I want? Simple. Karthik owes me—and my people—something. There's unfinished business between us. And until he pays for what he's done, he can't hide here, pretending to be some innocent villager."

Karthik's eyes locked onto Ananya's, and for a moment, everything else seemed to fade away. "Ananya, I won't let him drag you into this. I will protect you, no matter what."

Ananya, torn between love and fear, stepped back, her mind racing. She had seen Karthik's sincerity, had felt the change in him, but this was a part of his life that she couldn't ignore. Could she trust that he had truly left his past behind? Could she continue to build something with him, knowing that it might always be shadowed by what he had done?

"I need time, Karthik," she said softly, her voice filled with uncertainty. "I need time to understand this, to understand what it means for us."

Karthik's heart sank, but he nodded, understanding her need for space. "I'll give you all the time you need. But know this—whatever happens, I'll fight for you. I'll fight for us."

Arvind, seeing that his words had already caused enough damage, turned to leave, but not without a final, warning glance at Karthik. "This isn't over, Karthik. You can't run from your past forever."

As Arvind walked away, Ananya stood in silence, her heart torn between the man she had come to care for and the truth that threatened to pull them apart. Karthik had laid bare his past, but now, it was up to her to decide whether she could accept it and move forward—or if the weight of his past would prove too heavy to bear.

Chapter 16
A Moment of Reflection

The days that followed the confrontation between Karthik, Ananya, and Arvind felt like a blur. Ananya's heart was heavy with questions, her thoughts constantly swirling around Karthik's confession. She had seen his sincerity in the past, the way he had tried to make a fresh start, but could she truly believe that he had changed? Or was the man she had come to care for just another version of the person he used to be?

She spent hours walking through the village, trying to clear her mind, but the peaceful surroundings only seemed to deepen her confusion. The soft rustle of leaves in the trees, the distant chirping of birds, and the gentle hum of life in Sundarvan were at odds with the storm brewing inside her. She had always believed in second chances, in the possibility of redemption, but Karthik's past seemed like a shadow that would never lift.

Ananya found herself at the edge of the village, near the quiet stream where she had often gone to think. The cool breeze brushed against her face, and she closed her eyes, letting the calmness wash over her. But even here, she couldn't escape the turmoil inside.

Karthik had given her space, as he had promised, but the silence between them had only made things more difficult. She could feel his presence even when he wasn't near—his gaze always lingering on her, his actions trying to prove that he was worthy of her trust. But trust was fragile, and her heart was still unsure.

As she stood by the stream, lost in her thoughts, she heard the soft crunch of footsteps behind her. She turned, and there he was—Karthik, standing a few feet away, his face somber, his eyes filled with an emotion she couldn't quite place.

Ananya didn't speak immediately. Instead, she stared at him, waiting for him to break the silence. It had been days since they had spoken about what had happened with Arvind, and yet, there was so much left unspoken between them.

Karthik took a deep breath and stepped closer. "I know you need time, Ananya," he said quietly. "And I know I can't undo what I've done. I can't change the past, but I can promise you one thing: I'm here, and I'm not going anywhere."

Ananya felt a pang in her chest at his words. She had always admired his strength, his resilience. But this side of him, the vulnerability he was showing now, made her heart ache. "I want to believe you, Karthik," she said, her voice barely above a whisper. "But I don't know how."

Karthik's eyes searched hers, his expression softening with understanding. "I don't expect you to forgive me right away, Ananya. I know it's not that simple. But I need you to know that I'm not the same person I was. I've changed. And I will keep changing, for you, for us."

Ananya closed her eyes, the weight of his words pressing down on her. The truth was, she had never stopped caring for him. Despite everything, despite the secrets and the lies, she could still feel the pull toward him. But could love alone overcome the past?

She opened her eyes and looked at him. "I don't know if I can trust you again, Karthik. It's not just about your past, it's about what that means for us, for our future. I'm scared that one day, I'll find out there's more you're hiding, more you haven't told me."

Karthik took another step forward, his hand reaching out toward her, though he stopped just shy of touching her. "I won't hide anything from you, Ananya. Not anymore. I'll be open with you, no matter how hard it is. I won't let my past destroy what we have. Please… just give me a chance."

Ananya's heart fluttered at his words, but a part of her remained guarded. She had been hurt before, by others, by circumstances, and now, she feared that Karthik's past would be the one thing she couldn't overcome.

"I don't know if I can, Karthik," she murmured, tears threatening to spill from her eyes. "I want to, but I need time. I need to figure out what this all means."

Karthik nodded, his expression filled with sorrow, but he didn't press her further. He knew that pushing her would only make things harder. "Take all the time you need. I'll be here, waiting, no matter how long it takes."

The silence between them stretched on, but it wasn't the uncomfortable silence of before. It was filled with a sense of understanding, of unspoken words, and of hearts that were still connected despite the distance. Ananya took a deep breath and slowly nodded, feeling the weight of the decision she had to make.

"I'll think about it," she said softly, her voice trembling.

Karthik's face softened, a small but hopeful smile tugging at his lips. "That's all I can ask for."

And with that, he turned and walked away, leaving Ananya standing by the stream, her mind still heavy with doubt, but also with the smallest flicker of hope.

As the days passed, Ananya found herself reflecting on everything that had happened. She spent more time alone,

walking through the village, talking to her friends, and trying to understand what her heart was telling her. She knew she couldn't keep running from the truth, but she also knew that she couldn't let fear rule her decisions.

Karthik's words echoed in her mind, his promise of change and redemption. She wanted to believe in him, but the road ahead wasn't clear. What if she gave him a chance and he let her down again? What if his past caught up with him, pulling them both into something they couldn't escape?

As the sun began to set over Sundarvan, casting long shadows across the village, Ananya realized that the decision she faced wasn't just about Karthik. It was about her own journey, her own willingness to open her heart again, despite the scars of the past.

For the first time in days, she felt a sense of clarity. It wasn't about forgetting the past; it was about learning to live with it and choosing to move forward, together.

And so, with a heavy heart and a mind still full of questions, Ananya knew that the path ahead would be difficult. But it was a path she was willing to take, one step at a time.

Chapter 17

A Step Toward Trust

The days after their conversation by the stream passed in a haze. Ananya tried to focus on her daily routines, on her work, and on the life that had once felt so simple. But there was a constant undercurrent of thoughts about Karthik, about what had happened and what might be. His words echoed in her mind, and despite her fears, she found herself starting to let down her guard, little by little.

One afternoon, as Ananya was preparing a bouquet in her small shop, she heard the familiar sound of footsteps approaching. She glanced up and saw Karthik standing in the doorway, looking hesitant but determined.

Their eyes met, and for a moment, neither spoke. Ananya's heart quickened at the sight of him, but she kept her composure, focusing on the flowers in her hands.

"I know it's not easy," Karthik said, breaking the silence. "I don't expect you to make a decision right now. But I need you to know that I'm still here, Ananya. I'm not going anywhere."

Ananya paused, placing the flowers down slowly on the counter. Her mind was a whirlwind of emotions. She had been waiting for him to make the first move, to show her that he was serious, that he wasn't going to repeat the mistakes of his past.

"I've been thinking," Ananya said softly, looking up at him. "And I'm not ready to forgive you completely, not yet. But I can't ignore what I feel, either."

Karthik's face softened, a flicker of hope crossing his features. "I understand. I don't expect everything to be fixed in one moment. All I ask for is the chance to prove that I've changed. That I'm not the man I was before."

Ananya took a deep breath, her heart torn between caution and the desire to believe in him. "Trust is a fragile thing, Karthik," she said quietly. "I don't know if I can trust you right now. But I'm willing to try."

The words hung in the air between them, heavy with significance. Karthik nodded, understanding the weight of her decision. "I'll take it, Ananya. I'll take whatever you're willing to give, and I'll prove to you that I'm worthy of your trust."

Ananya's thoughts swirled as she looked into his eyes, seeing both vulnerability and sincerity. She didn't know where this journey would lead, but for the first time in a long time, she felt like she was taking a step toward something real, something worth fighting for.

"Let's take it slow," she said, her voice gentle but firm. "One step at a time. No pressure, no expectations. Just... time."

Karthik smiled, a genuine smile that reached his eyes. "One step at a time. I can do that."

The next few days were filled with small moments of reconnection. Karthik was patient, giving Ananya the space she needed while showing her through his actions that he was committed to earning back her trust. They shared simple, quiet moments—sitting in the garden as the sun set, talking about their dreams, their fears, their pasts. The weight of their history was always there, lingering in the background, but slowly, the present was beginning to feel more important.

Ananya noticed the changes in Karthik—how he had started to share more of himself with her, how he had been

open about his regrets and the lessons he had learned. She could see the sincerity in his eyes, hear the vulnerability in his voice, and yet, a part of her still held back, unsure if this transformation was permanent.

But as the days turned into weeks, Ananya found herself allowing Karthik in, bit by bit. She began to trust his words, his actions, his intentions. It was still a fragile trust, but it was growing. The past was still there, hovering at the edges of their relationship, but it no longer seemed like an insurmountable barrier.

One evening, as they sat together by the garden, watching the stars, Karthik turned to Ananya with a quiet determination in his eyes.

"I know it's been hard for you to let me back in," he said softly. "But I promise you, Ananya, I'm not going to hurt you. I'm not going to make the same mistakes again."

Ananya turned to face him, her heart pounding in her chest. She had heard him say this before, but now, something in his voice made her believe him.

"I know," she whispered, her voice barely audible. "I believe you."

And for the first time in a long time, Ananya allowed herself to feel something she hadn't felt in a while—hope. She didn't know what the future held, but she was willing to take that next step with Karthik, trusting that together, they could build something new

Chapter 18
A TEST OF FAITH

The days turned into weeks, and the soft tension between Ananya and Karthik seemed to dissipate with every passing moment. Their relationship, though still fragile, had grown into something more comfortable—more honest. They spent more time together, walking through the village, sharing stories of their childhoods, and slowly unearthing the scars they had both carried for so long. Karthik's commitment to change was evident in the small, thoughtful things he did. He never rushed Ananya; he never pressured her for more than she was ready to give.

Yet, as the bond between them deepened, Ananya still struggled with the lingering fear of being hurt again. Every time Karthik reached out, every time he shared a part of himself, she couldn't help but wonder if his transformation was real or if it was just a fleeting attempt to win back her trust. She was walking a fine line between hope and caution.

One evening, as the golden hues of the sunset bathed the village in a serene glow, Ananya found herself at the local market, buying fresh flowers for the shop. The air was cool, and the sounds of evening chatter filled the streets. As she browsed the stalls, she suddenly heard a voice call out her name.

"Ananya!"

Turning around, she saw her childhood friend, Priya, walking toward her with a wide smile. Priya had recently moved back to Sundarvan after a few years spent in the city. She was the

kind of person who never held back, always speaking her mind and living with an infectious energy.

"Priya! It's so good to see you!" Ananya said, smiling warmly as they embraced.

"I know, it's been ages!" Priya replied, laughing. "I just moved back a couple of weeks ago. I've been meaning to catch up with you. How are you? And, more importantly, how's the mysterious Karthik doing?"

Ananya felt a sudden pang in her chest at the mention of Karthik. It wasn't that she didn't want to talk about him, but something about Priya's probing question made her uneasy.

"Well, things are... better," Ananya said cautiously, picking up a bouquet of lilies from the stall. "We're taking things slow, one step at a time."

Priya raised an eyebrow. "Taking things slow? Or are you just being cautious?"

Ananya hesitated. "A bit of both, I suppose."

Priya watched her carefully, sensing the deeper unease in her friend's tone. "I get it. You're scared. But you have to ask yourself, Ananya—are you holding back because of the past, or because something in the present is making you doubt him?"

Ananya's heart skipped a beat at the question. She had asked herself that very thing a thousand times. Was she afraid of repeating history, of making the same mistakes? Or was Karthik truly different this time? The uncertainty felt suffocating.

"I don't know," Ananya admitted, her voice barely a whisper. "I want to believe he's changed, but there's still so

much I don't know. So much about his past... about things he hasn't told me."

Priya's expression softened, and she reached out to place a hand on Ananya's shoulder. "I know it's scary, Ananya. But the past doesn't have to define the future. You're not the same person you were when you were younger, right? Neither is he. People change, and sometimes, we have to let go of our fears to let that change take root."

Ananya nodded slowly, her mind racing with conflicting emotions. It was true—she had changed. She was no longer the naive girl who believed that love could conquer all. But perhaps she had also become someone who was too afraid to trust, to risk opening herself up to love again. Could she afford to live in the shadows of what might go wrong, or could she embrace the possibility of something new?

As she stood there with Priya, the weight of her internal struggle grew heavier. She knew she had to make a decision, and soon. If she kept holding onto the past, she might lose the present. And if she didn't take a leap of faith, she might never know what could have been with Karthik.

The next few days were a whirlwind of emotions for Ananya. She continued to reflect on her conversation with Priya and the questions that had been lingering in her heart. Every time she saw Karthik, the gentle sincerity in his eyes made her want to believe in him. But the fear of disappointment, the fear of being betrayed again, kept her at a distance.

Then, one evening, as she walked home from the market, she saw Karthik waiting for her by the old oak tree in the village square. He was leaning against the trunk, looking thoughtful, his hands in his pockets. The sight of him, standing there alone, waiting for her, made her heart flutter.

As she approached him, Karthik straightened, his eyes lighting up when he saw her. "Ananya," he said, his voice soft, "I've been thinking a lot about us... about everything. I know I can't ask you to trust me right away, but I need you to know that I'm willing to do whatever it takes to earn that trust. To prove to you that I'm here for you, for us."

Ananya stopped in front of him, her heart racing. She could see the sincerity in his expression, the vulnerability that had always been there beneath his tough exterior. But was it enough?

"I know," she said slowly, her voice trembling. "I know you're trying, Karthik. But I need to ask myself, too. I need to decide if I'm ready to take that step. If I'm ready to trust you again."

Karthik nodded, his gaze unwavering. "Take all the time you need, Ananya. I'm not going anywhere. I'll be here, no matter how long it takes."

Ananya took a deep breath, her heart heavy with the weight of the decision ahead. She knew that trusting Karthik again wasn't going to be easy. It would take time, effort, and a leap of faith—one that she wasn't sure she was ready to take. But as she looked at him, standing before her, waiting patiently, she realized that sometimes, taking a step toward trust was the only way to move forward.

Chapter 19

A Leap of Faith

The cool evening breeze whispered through the trees as Ananya stood by the old oak tree, her mind a swirl of thoughts. She had spent countless nights pondering the same questions: Was she ready to take the leap? Could she truly trust Karthik again, after everything that had happened? The fear that had gripped her heart for so long still lingered, but there was something else now—a flicker of hope, a quiet voice telling her that maybe, just maybe, it was worth the risk.

Karthik stood before her, waiting patiently, his face calm but his eyes betraying the hope and uncertainty he felt. He had laid his heart bare for her, telling her how much he wanted to rebuild what they had lost, but he also knew that he couldn't rush her. He had to wait until she was ready.

"I've been thinking a lot, Karthik," Ananya finally spoke, her voice soft but steady. "And I realized something important. I've been holding onto the past for so long, trying to protect myself from the possibility of getting hurt again. But I can't keep living like this. I can't keep letting fear control my choices."

Karthik's eyes lit up, a cautious smile tugging at his lips, but he didn't interrupt. He simply waited for her to continue.

"I'm scared," Ananya continued, her hands nervously folding and unfolding in front of her. "Scared that I'll end up disappointed, scared that I'll lose myself in something that could break me. But I know that if I don't take a chance, I'll never know what could be. I'll never know if we can have something real."

Karthik took a step forward, his voice low but earnest. "Ananya, I understand your fear. I can't promise that everything will be perfect, that we won't face challenges. But what I can promise is that I'll always be here, doing everything I can to make things right, to be the person you deserve."

Ananya took a deep breath, her heart racing as she finally looked up into his eyes. She could see the sincerity there, the determination that matched her own desire to move forward. The walls she had built around herself began to crack, and for the first time in a long while, she felt like she could breathe, like she could believe in something greater than her fear.

"I'm ready," she said quietly, her voice steady. "I'm ready to trust you, Karthik. I'm ready to take the leap."

Karthik's expression softened, and a wave of emotion passed over him. He reached out and gently took her hands in his, holding them with a tenderness that spoke volumes. "Thank you," he whispered. "I won't let you down. I promise."

As the last light of day faded, they stood there together, the night air wrapping around them like a blanket. The uncertainty that had once felt so overwhelming was now replaced by something lighter, something more hopeful. Ananya didn't know what the future held, but for the first time, she felt like she was walking into it with Karthik by her side.

The next few weeks felt like a new chapter for Ananya and Karthik. They were still taking things slowly, allowing their connection to grow without the pressure of expectations. Ananya had learned to embrace the uncertainty of love, to trust in the process rather than demand immediate answers. She allowed herself to feel vulnerable, to open up in ways she hadn't in years, and with every moment, her trust in Karthik deepened.

They spent their days exploring the village together, rediscovering the places they had once known, but with fresh eyes. The simple acts of sharing a meal, taking a walk under the stars, and talking about their hopes for the future filled the spaces between them with a warmth that felt like home.

One evening, as they sat together in the small garden outside her house, the soft glow of lanterns flickering around them, Karthik looked at Ananya with a tenderness that made her heart skip a beat.

"You know," he began, his voice low and thoughtful, "I never thought I'd get a second chance like this. To make things right, to show you who I really am. I don't take it lightly, Ananya."

Ananya turned to him, her eyes soft with understanding. "You've already shown me, Karthik. In everything you've done, in the way you've been there for me. I see the man you've become, and I'm proud of you."

Karthik smiled, a mixture of relief and gratitude flooding his expression. "And I'm proud of you, too. For trusting me again. For letting go of the past."

They sat in silence for a few moments, the sound of crickets chirping in the background and the rustling of leaves in the trees. Ananya leaned her head on his shoulder, feeling the steady beat of his heart beneath her cheek.

For the first time in a long time, Ananya felt at peace. She had taken the leap, and though there would still be challenges ahead, she knew that with Karthik, they could face them together. The past no longer had a hold on her; it was the present, the now, that mattered. And in this moment, she was exactly where she needed to be.

ABOUT THE AUTHOR –

Soumen Sengupta

Soumen Sengupta is a storyteller at heart, weaving narratives that explore love, longing, and the complexities of human emotions. His latest work, The Heart's Trilogy, is a collection of three deeply evocative stories — The Midnight Letter, The Quiet Goodbye, and The Canvas of Heart — each capturing the essence of relationships, self-discovery, and the power of unspoken words.

A lifelong diary writer, Soumen's passion for storytelling began in childhood, shaping his ability to craft heartfelt and immersive tales. His writing is known for its emotional depth, relatable characters, and poetic prose, resonating with readers who seek stories that linger long after the last page.

With The Heart's Trilogy, Soumen invites readers into a world where love is both a solace and a journey—one that unfolds through quiet moments, whispered confessions, and the courage to embrace change.

When he's not writing, Soumen is busy nurturing his publication house, offering a platform for emerging writers. Through his work, he continues to inspire, reminding us that every heart holds a story worth telling.

Thank you!

9 789358 231687

Printed at Repro India Ltd.